IN FLESH AND STONE

by Hal Bodner

"There are these... things," Alex fought his reluctance to share something so deeply personal. "They're statues. I suppose you might call them gargoyles of a sort. Twelve of them. One for each sign of the zodiac. That's what I call them. The Zodiac Men."

Once again, he could see them, their smooth marble flesh glowing in the vestiges of light from the setting sun, stray beams seeping past the grime-covered skylight. Each one was more beautiful than the one before. If only they were real! If only by some miracle their cold and gleaming flesh could become warm and supple. Alex longed to feel the heat of their bodies beneath his fingers, to savor the saltiness of their skin upon his tongue, to inhale the raw, musky maleness of their scent.

But no. They were cold, cold marble. And what Alex had thought he'd seen, that slight, elusive flicker of movement, was nothing but the playful teasing of his frustrated libido and over-active imagination.

Or was it?

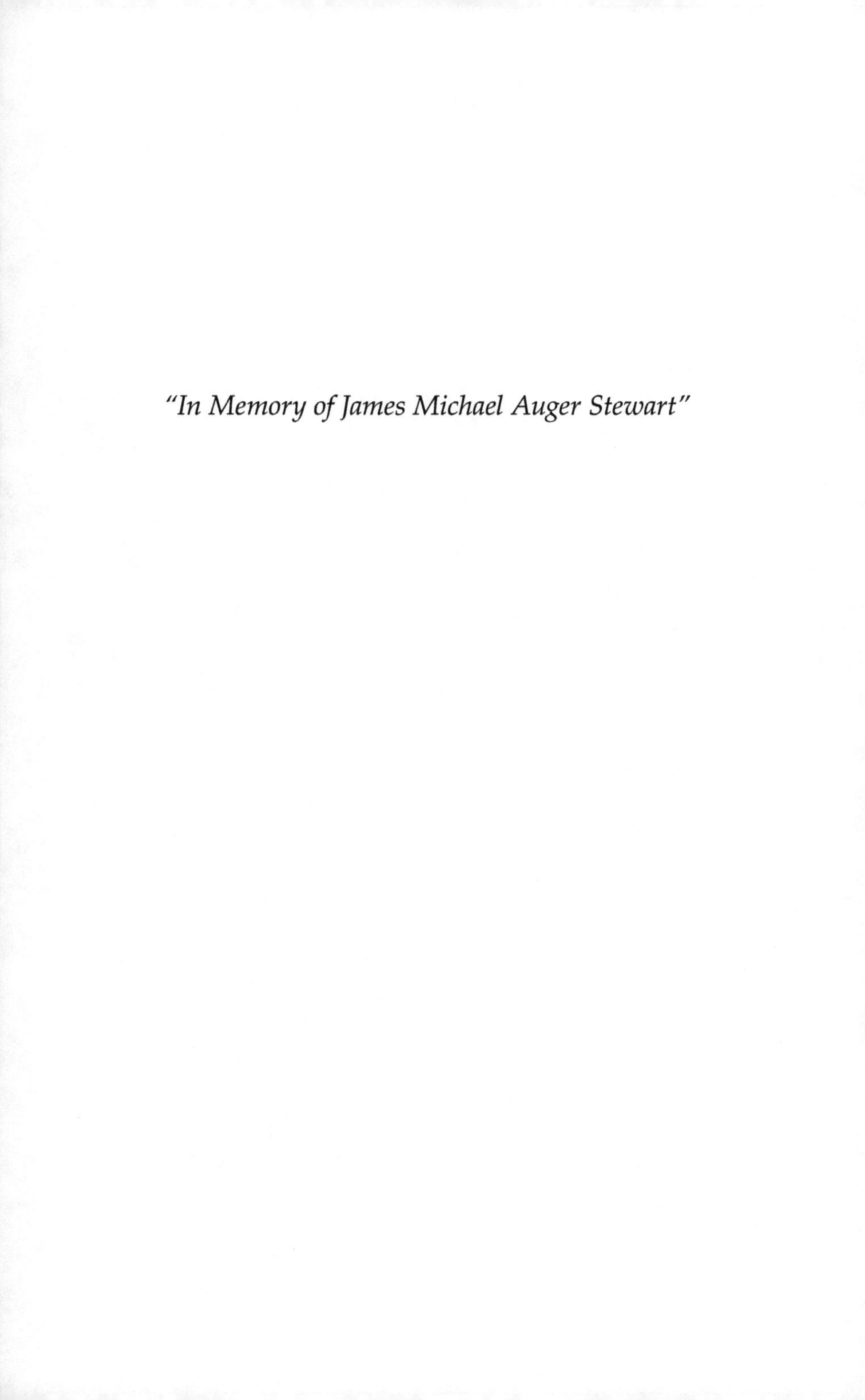

"In Memory of James Michael Auger Stewart"

CHAPTER 1

The only time Alex could remember being surrounded by so many naked dicks was many years ago in the steam room at the gym. He'd been younger then, certainly more limber and ever so much more eager to please. Even now, after all this time, the recollection brought a flush of mingled pleasure and shame to his cheeks – with not a little pride at his versatility and accomplished skill thrown in for good measure.

Ah! The nights of drinking and dancing until the bars closed at two in the morning, with the occasional toot thrown in—but only if the trick insisted and was exceptionally hot. Alex had never been one for drugs. Alcohol, of course, was another matter. Recently, his fridge had been converted into the quintessential larder of a gay bachelor: a jar of peanut butter, a few lemons which had moved past their prime before he could use them, various protein powder canisters, a few light beers and an unopened bag of organic greens. The rest of the shelves were practically bare except for bottle each of club soda and tonic water and two cans of diet cola, the residue of a container of low-fat dressing and some half-eaten sandwiches in doggy bags from nearby restaurants. Not to be overlooked was the quart of Stoli chilling in the freezer compartment. It was conveniently stashed next to an ancient package of boneless, skinless chicken breasts he'd bought to save money by cooking at home, but had somehow never gotten around to.

Not to say there hadn't been times, not too long ago, when the fridge had been replete with delicacies and the makings for healthy dinners for two. But the one constant had always been the cold vodka next to the ice cube tray.

His mind wandered away from the contents of his fridge

and back to the party days of his halcyon youth. Doubtless, the dicks staring him in the face had something to do with the redirection of his memory.

Back then, once the bouncers had finished ushering out the stragglers and patrolling the restrooms to make sure no one had either collapsed in the stalls from an overdose or, more commonly, had decided to skip getting a motel room in favor of sucking off a trick on top of the commode, the doors of the bar would be locked and chained. Then, the night would truly begin.

Hollywood boasted a smattering of after-hours gay clubs. Sometimes, they could be fun and, the few times he'd gone, Alex had met some very interesting young men who had proven to be equally as interested in him. But state law prohibited the sale of booze after the bars closed and, frankly, Alex had always found that social intercourse, and other types of intercourse as well, always went more smoothly and was made much easier when lubricated by a dry martini or Sea Breeze. The local bathhouse might have been an option, but Alex had preconceived notions of dark corridors suffused with the smell of mildew and cheap disinfectant, populated by extraordinarily skinny or hugely obese lecherous old codgers with more hair on their backs than on their heads, arms grasping to seize Alex's toned and muscled body and drag him into the depths of their cubicles for God only knew what, nevermore to see the light of day.

Of course, that was before he'd met Tony.

Things changed when you got married. You still got to witness the dawn once in a while, but it was usually because you and your husband were getting up before sunrise in order to catch a plane for a well-earned vacation in Hawaii and not because you were stumbling in still drunk from the night before. You started to think less about things like maintaining your social circle of people who, while they might be physically attractive, you didn't really like, and you started looking at the Ikea catalogue in a new light and paying attention to the Year End Savings Sales at Macy's to see if they had reduced the price on the couch you and your spouse had been lusting for. You even—perish the thought—started to pay attention to that little voice in your head that whispered, "You already have a husband, right? So, why are you still spending so much time in the gym? Twice a week is enough to keep things looking good without going overboard. Besides, he says he likes you better with a little extra meat on your bones."

You got comfortable.

But the comfort was gone, vanished like the days of partying until he could barely walk. At the moment, Alex didn't have the emotional fortitude to start searching for a new companion, and he sure as hell knew he didn't have the physical capacity nor the flexibility to abuse his body like he once could.

Instead, he stood surrounded by dicks.

There were twelve of them. Thirteen, actually, if he counted the twins, and he *definitely* counted the twins. Some were fully erect, slim and mushroom headed, ridged with throbbing veins. A few were barely tumescent but showed impressive promise. The longest was—and Alex prided himself on being an excellent judge in matters of this importance—very close to twelve inches, with a head that could only be described as eagerly perky. The shortest was tougher to estimate, being only semi-erect, but Alex suspected the startling heft and thickness of the thing would more than make up for any lack of the distance it could penetrate. Most, Alex suspected, were not circumcised, but insofar as those dicks most prominently displayed were concerned, the foreskin had been gathered where the shaft met the head—so it was hard to tell for sure.

They were, quite possibly, thirteen of the most magnificent dicks Alex had ever seen—and the bodies attached to the dicks were nothing to sneeze at either.

Though the twins had far from the most spectacular physiques of the group, Alex found himself drawn to them more than to the others. He doubted he'd have been able to imagine two physical specimens of young manhood more his "type" than they were. Besides, there were *two* of them, identically beautiful, and even the passing fancy of what kinds of erotic tripods could result from *that* combination made Alex's shorts uncomfortably tight. They were obviously natural athletes; he envisioned them stripped to loincloths, their oiled bodies sweating under the broiling Mediterranean sun of some ancient Greek Olympic field, muscles straining as they threw javelins or hurled the discus in perfect synchronicity. Better yet, he pictured them completely naked—and since they were already naked, his creative juices weren't taxed too hard to form the mental picture—sweating in some sandy arena while they wrestled, sun-bronzed arms and legs intertwined, chests heaving with grunts of effort, bits of dirt clinging artistically to perspiration-soaked shoulders and backs. They stood, each with an arm draped casually around his brother's shoulder, shyly smiling at Alex with expressions hinting of erotic delights that could only be performed in groups of more than two.

The other eleven men were all in their own unique ways equally stunning. Even the hirsute, thick-chested fellow in the corner with the shoulders of a linebacker and the humongous dick proudly at attention in a field of lush, wiry dark hair-covered legs and a veritable forest of crotch—though Alex was not normally attracted to guys who weren't smooth, or at the least trimmed or shaved—even he was someone Alex would be loath to kick out of bed for eating crackers. More likely, he'd do whatever was most likely to get him into bed in the first place—up to and including sacrificing his first-born child to some pagan god of lust, were he ever to consider having a kid.

Certainly, there was enough variety of male flesh to keep him entertained for months. Broad, heavy chests, manly chests, sheathed with muscle and tipped with large, full nipples to suckle at. Slim, wasp-waisted younger men, with tapered V-shapes, washboard stomachs and what Alex thought of as "poppy seed nipples" to be teased and licked. Impressive shoulders and massive biceps strong enough to lift him clean off his feet, cradle him in strong arms and carry him to some erotic orgy before overpowering him with such force that Alex would only be able to bite the pillow and moan as the weight of his lover forced him deeper into the mattress. Lithe, dancer builds, all smooth skin and flexibility so Alex would want to be the aggressor and guide the young athlete into new contortions, experimenting with novel positions where arms and legs could stretch and twist to reach all sorts of interesting places—and occupy themselves with even *more* interesting titillation.

And the faces! Even the few older men—perhaps nearing forty—were exquisitely beautiful. Whether he was grinning at the youngest of the bunch, a youth of barely twenty with almond eyes, thin lips bearing the start of a shy smile and a sharp, angled jaw evoking some wood sprite lurking in the foliage of an enchanted forest, eager for naked playtime, or if he was distracted by the craggy handsomeness of the more mature daddy-type with all the hair below the waist, Alex could scarce find a single flaw in any of the men's perfection. Such magnificent nudity, such an overload of perfectly honed bodies, such raw sensuality...well, Alex had been pretty much operating on auto-pilot since he first entered the room and saw them.

As for his own dick? Evidently, its auto-pilot had already shifted into overdrive.

Alex glanced down at his cotton shorts and regretted having decided not to change after his morning jog. He'd figured, with so much work to do today, a lot of it likely to involve a substantial amount of sweat and grime, he'd might as well not have to soil an extra pair for the laundry. But he hadn't counted on the reaction the thirteen stunning men were producing. He was leaking like a sieve, his jock strap was already soaked through and, he feared, the pre-cum would very shortly work its way through the running shorts themselves to display itself.

Hopefully, over the next few hours, he could work up enough of a sweat to hide the telltale signs of his arousal.

He took a last, lingering look at the dicks, making sure to take in as many details of each for later consideration as he could, and sighed. Sadly, Alex knew he'd have plenty of time to closely examine every inch of them in the coming weeks.

For the foreseeable future, these thirteen statues would be his only companions and would provide his only erotic release.

There was a muffled curse from the doorway, followed by a string of much more audible cursing and a thump. Alex winced at the sound of a wooden crate hitting the marble floor and hoped nothing had been damaged.

"Jesus, Alex! I thought you were going to help me with all

this sh…" The voice of the young man trailed off as he caught his first glimpse of the dicks. "Wow!" Midnight blue eyes sparkled with something akin to lust as the shirtless, dark auburn-haired young man took in the details. "*This* is your new apartment?"

Alex couldn't suppress a grin, tinged with just the tiniest bit of embarrassment that he'd been caught. "Yeah. It's great, isn't it?"

"I'll say! It sure as hell beats porn any day. Although…" The man in the doorway frowned at the statues. "…it's not like they can actually…perform, is it?"

"That, my dear Corey, is one of the truly sad things in the universe."

Corey craned his neck to examine the thirteen men in awe. "How the heck did they get here?" He pointed. "I think that one's my favorite. I'd do him in a bar any day. Hell, I'd do him in Macy's window if I got the chance."

Alex's eyes followed the line of Corey's finger. "That's Aries, I think. Wait, no. Taurus. You always did have a thing for older guys with big balls."

"Daddy, Daddy!" Corey's head bobbed enthusiastically. "Bull balls. Lemme at 'em."

"I kind of like Gemini myself."

"Knowing you, that's a surprise?"

Corey scratched an itch on his chest with studied idleness. Alex wasn't fooled for a minute. The way Corey's fingers kept brushing his own nipple while he scratched, the way they lightly flicked over the sparse hair surrounding the aureole, Alex knew the movement was anything but casual. With his next words, Corey confirmed Alex's suspicions.

"You may be my age, but I never had a problem with *your* balls, if you can remember that long ago." Corey's grin was practically a leer. It was abundantly clear what he wanted.

Their time together as regular lovers had come and gone a long time ago; they'd been college roommates at the time. The finale had come about, not because of any fading of attraction, but simply because Tony had come into Alex's life. Corey was good sex. Hell, he was pretty amazing sex, actually. But with Tony, there had been more—there still was more. With Tony, there was love.

Still, Corey was standing there making his desires known and Tony was obviously not available. He considered. Bedding Corey—or rather flooring Corey, as the bed was still packed in the truck—would be a solution of sorts. Even when he and Tony were together and ostensibly monogamous, or at least more monogamous than most gay couples, Tony had always tolerated a special dispensation for Corey. Tony knew Alex and Corey had been lovers of convenience for four years; Alex had hidden nothing. Tony also realized the close friendship between the two had developed independently of the sex. Corey was just too damned easy to like and the very qualities that made him such a great companion, Tony had intuited, were the ones that made it impossible for Alex and Corey to ever have a more meaningful intimate relationship.

Corey took nothing seriously—except sex, parties and the gym. He was one of those beautiful youngish gay men whose wallet was always full enough to pay the cover and stand for a round of drinks, yet never seemed to have any permanent gainful employment. Normally, Alex would have suspected a sugar daddy lurked somewhere in Corey's background, but he knew better. There had been gifts from admirers, of course, some of them quite expensive. The truck they'd used to move Alex's belongings was one such present. Most of them though, came in the form of trips to exotic locations, fancy dinners and overpriced clothing. Having spent many hours at Corey's apartment, Alex knew the dresser drawers were brimming with overpriced trendy labeled underwear and swimsuits, the closets were packed full of tight shirts and even tighter jeans, all of them purchased for him by men who took great delight in having Corey model them for him in the clothing stores. The watches and jewelry Corey generally returned or, if he didn't know where his latest beau had originally bought them, pawned for whatever he could get.

It netted enough, Alex supposed, for Corey to get by so long as he supplemented his income with the occasional cater-waiter job or a stint posing at photo shoots for one of the ubiquitous skin mags. For a while, Corey had dabbled in online Web cam sex. It may have been the only time the redhead had ever made consistently decent money in his life. But, having to have sex on camera at predesignated times, Corey had confessed, simply bored the crap out of him and, as he had put it, cramped his style. He'd done two porno films but was disenchanted almost immediately and complained that on-camera sex was mostly about angles and lighting and not very much fun at all. Though Corey's two titles were still selling very well and Corey had been offered what seemed to Alex to be an exorbitant amount of money to be naked and have sex with hot strangers on camera, he had consistently declined.

Alex took a long moment to let his eyes rove up and down Corey's body. It was well-muscled from long days spent working out at the gym, and the hours on the stair machine and stationary bike had certainly paid off; there was nary an ounce of body fat on him. His belly was cut like one of those suits of body armor Hollywood costumers were so fond of putting on cinema superheroes, and the striations of his shoulder muscles and back were clearly visible through the skin—and through most of the skin tight shirts he wore when he deigned to wear a shirt in the first place. A compact torso with a smattering of sun-bleached hair on the chest, descending in a pleasure trail down his stomach completed the picture of his upper body.

Corey knew damned well Alex was drinking him in with his eyes and sought to tempt him further. He clasped his fingers together behind his head in a calculated stretch, showing off the V-shape of his torso and arching his back to force the muscles of his chest into greater definition. His nipples were hard from the attention his fingers had been giving them a moment earlier and, he knew, twin trickles of sweat wound their way from his armpits down his sides toward the waistband of his low-hanging cut-off shorts. He moved one foot slightly forward, intentionally flexing his thigh to make every cut stand out, unconsciously striking a pose that would have fit in well with the thirteen statues lining the walls.

"It's been a long time," Corey whispered. "Look, I'm even sweating. You know how much you like that."

Alex swallowed to moisten his throat, suddenly grown dry. It was true. Corey was one of those guys who, in spite of a head of hair that tended towards red, had been gifted with dark, thick skin that tanned to a golden bronze. He spent days at the beach, oiled up and broiling in the sun, coming home to lather himself with moisturizer so his skin stayed supple and smooth. He was also one of those lucky people who, however much they might sweat from heat or exertion—and Corey perspired liberally—never gave off a rank odor. Alex remembered many a college afternoon or evening spent naked in bed while licking the salty fluid from his roommate's body, delaying the moment when he could bury his face in the pit of Corey's arms, at the precise spot where the muscles of his back met his sides, and languorously breathe in the scent of him, musky and wholesome, with just a touch of something wild and earthy. The smell of Corey's body—now that it had sprung to mind, Alex imagined he could sense it even while standing several feet away—was usually enough to encourage his dick to swell even further.

"Is that for me?" Corey feigned surprise, blinking his eyelashes in a parody of a coquette, his gazed fixed on the telltale bulge in Alex's shorts.

Alex was about to move forward, to doff his own shirt in a single motion to press his own chest against Corey's naked flesh and dive right in, but at the last moment, he hesitated. Sadness washed over him.

Instantly, Cory abandoned all salaciousness and was at his side, fingers kneading Alex's shoulders, comforting him as the waterworks started.

"Aw, Jesus, Alex. I'm sorry. I didn't think."

"No, that's okay." Alex choked back the sobs and turned into Corey's embrace, hugging him without any sensuality, just to let him know he was forgiven.

"You know," Corey said, stroking Alex's honey brown hair to soothe him. "You're gonna have needs, buddy boy. At some point, you're gonna give in to 'em. At least with me, you don't have all that guilt about being unfaithful. Tony wouldn't mind."

"I can't. Not just yet."

Corey kissed him gently on the forehead, slowly moving his mouth down across his face, licking up the remains of his tears, finally teasing at the corners of Alex's lips with the tip of his tongue. Alex opened his mouth and, without volition, moaned and Corey was quick to take advantage of the movement, sealing Alex's mouth with his, tongue probing until he felt his slightly shorter friend's body shudder.

All of Alex's resistance fled. He sagged into Corey's chest, breaking the kiss so his tongue was free to move about his friend's upper body. He licked his upper chest, hungrily sucking at Corey's large nipples, biting the tips gently as he knew Corey liked. All the while his hands roved Corey's back, grasping and kneading at the muscles on either side of his backbone, finally coming to rest with two handfuls of taut, hard-muscled ass, squeezing and prodding the mounds.

"You need this, baby," Corey murmured. "You really, really do."

"There's…there's nothing…" Alex gasped, then to clarify, "No bed. No furniture."

Corey just smiled and, with the ease of long practice, flipped the front of Alex's T-shirt over his head, baring his chest but leaving his arms still in the sleeves and his upper back still covered with cloth.

"If I remember…," Corey began playfully. He ran the backs of his hands over Alex's naked flesh lightly, barely disturbing the fine, almost invisible hairs, circling the slabs of his chest, brushing the tips of the nipples until he elicited a moan before moving lower. Wiggling his fingers like he was mimicking a spider crawling, or playing the keys of a phantom piano, he lightly tickled Alex's stomach and upper groin. Finally, he began playing with the sparse hair just below Alex's navel, tugging the hairs gently one by one while his friend gasped. "…this is something you like. Or did I get it wrong?"

"No!" Alex managed to blurt. "It's right. Damn! It's *so* right."

So skillfully that Alex didn't know what had happened until the cooler air of the room caused goose bumps on his upper groin, Corey undid the button on Alex's shorts and unzipped the fly to expose the soaked-through jock.

"My, my! What have we here?" Corey teased.

He gently guided Alex a few steps until his back was pressed against the wall, not bothering to remove his T-shirt completely. He knelt, rolling the cotton shorts down Alex's legs, making sure his hands stayed in contact to tickle the hairs on the way down, until they were lying around his ankles. Then he sat back on his heels to enjoy the view.

Alex stood leaning against the wall, shirt bunched at his shoulders, chest bared and heaving, naked down to his ankles except for the jock strap.

"Hot!" was Corey's only comment before he leaned forward to nuzzle at Alex's cotton-covered dick, nipping the material and some of the flesh beneath lightly, tantalizing for a few long moments while Alex made involuntary guttural noises in the back of his throat. With his teeth, Corey latched onto the elastic band and, drawing it out an inch, allowed it to snap back and was rewarded when Alex arched forward and remained standing only because the tops of his shoulders were still against the wall. An instant later, his body slammed back against the smooth expanse of paneling and he cried out.

"Not yet." Corey looked up, his face split by a mischievous grin. "I'm just getting started."

He attacked the bulge in Alex's jockstrap anew, using teeth and lips and tongue with consummate skill honed by years of doing the exact same thing to the endless progression of models, wannabe actors and personal trainers who made up his usual sex partners. He could taste Alex's sweat from his earlier jog in the cloth, salty and sharp, musky and warm. Had his mouth not been occupied, he would have smiled at the other flavor he knew so well, the vaguely woodsy, almost mushroom taste of pre-cum. Alex's ability to shoot prodigious loads after hours of leaking was one of Corey's most cherished rewards for teasing him for as long as he possibly could.

Corey regretted this was not one of those times. Though he would have loved the chance to stretch this out for the rest of the day, Alex was in no condition to withstand that kind of treatment. Besides, they had to finish moving him into the new apartment. Nevertheless, there was no point in moving things to the finish too quickly. Corey would take his time and enjoy himself.

In very short order, the jockstrap was dripping wet with

a combination of Corey's saliva and the forerunners of Alex's sperm. When he judged the time was right, he used his teeth to grasp the jock and free the blond's throbbing penis to leap and bob, seeking any friction that would allow release. At the same time, he reached into his own waistband and skillfully rolled down his shorts—unlike Alex, he never wore anything underneath—to reveal his own pulsing erection.

With one hand, he grasped his cock, stroking it with increasing speed; the other snaked around to Alex's rear, toying with the hairs on his friend's ass, lubricating his fingers with Alex's sweat. Slowly, he teased the indentation of Alex's hole, circling the opening, feeling the blood pulsing in the tender tissue, his nails scratching lightly at the sensitive skin. It wasn't long before Corey felt what he'd been waiting for, the slight spasmodic pucker and widening of Alex's hole.

Corey smiled, and attacked. He thrust two fingers into Alex's gaping hole. At the same instant, he opened his mouth wide and, in a second, he had wrapped his mouth around Alex's pulsing cock, swallowing the full length of it, feeling the warm throb at the back of his throat. Alex cried out, an inarticulate primal sound, and clenched his fingers in Corey's hair. Thrusting helplessly, he toppled forward, bearing Corey to the marble floor, pumping and moaning while Corey's talented fingers probed even more deeply into his asshole, fucking his face with movements like a lascivious rodeo star trying to stay astride a bucking bull.

Corey loved the taste and feel of Alex's cock in his mouth; he always found it strangely comforting, a familiar emotional sensation from his carefree past. He guessed the warm inner glow he felt was akin to what some people experienced when they smelled fresh baked brownies which took them back to their childhood. In Corey's case, the salty hot maleness transported him back to college when he didn't need to concern himself with mundane trivialities like making a living. No, it was a happier time, when his only concerns were how quickly he could manage to screw the quarterback or the majority of the boys' swim team.

He felt the pulse of Alex's cock—which had always been prone to a peculiar throb just before it actually shot—and knew

Alex was about to climax. Eagerly, he increased the pace on his own cock and was rewarded. Gasping, thrashing and heaving, their climaxes were virtually simultaneous. A thick ribbon of milky white sperm shot from Corey's dick in a long stream, splattering onto the floor between Alex's feet. Corey's jaws and neck ached from the effort of trying to still move his mouth up and down the shaft at the same time he was swallowing. Closing his throat to prolong things and squeeze the last few spasmed drops from Alex's still-hard dick, Corey regretted only that the moment of climax was too quickly passed. He longed to extend it, in delicious stasis, for ever and ever.

Though he had been with more beautiful men in his time, and though he knew he and Alex would never be more than good friends with benefits, having sex with Alex was the only time he felt truly safe. Physically, in spite of the emotional incompatibility they'd experienced as bona fide lovers, they had always somehow…fit.

Collapsed in the contented afterglow, the two lay intertwined, each lost in his own thoughts. For Corey, his mind toyed with the fantasy that he and Alex would spend the rest of their lives together, living as partners, sharing their physical delights with each of them pushing the erotic buttons of the other, buttons they both knew all too well. Finally, he disentangled his limbs, rolled over onto his stomach and came back to reality.

It would never work. He and Alex knew each other too well, better perhaps than two people should. No matter how much they both might wish a relationship with each other, they had already tried it and it hadn't worked. They loved each other deeply, and they certainly stoked the passion in each other's bodies. But it was not a romantic love and the passion was of the moment, a flame too hot to be indefinitely extended.

As for what Alex was thinking, Corey would have been a little shocked that maybe he didn't know his best friend quite as well as he'd assumed.

Spent from the physical sensations, Alex looked up, allowing his mind to wander. But the scope of his thoughts stayed within a narrow range. It could even be numbered and the number was thirteen.

His eyes roved over the smooth marble of the statues, taking in the strange characteristics of each. The large round testicles and bulging penis balanced on Libra's scales, the horns on the head of hairy-bodied Taurus and the just-this-shy-of-overly-muscled Aries, the sleek equine flanks of Capricorn and Sagittarius, and the sly knowing smiles of the Gemini, whose free hands, from this angle, cupped each other's genitals.

Alex drank in each detail, marveling at the not-so-subtle eroticism the sculptor had evoked from each figure. He wondered how the statues had been allowed to stand in public view back in the days before the old library had been closed down, partitioned up and converted into condo lofts. He longed for the talent to sculpt such heavenly beings and, though his own artistic ability with brushes and oils was not insubstantial, he regretted never having been inspired to such creative heights with hammer and chisel.

He looked at the zodiac gods of male perfection with awe, as if witnessing an unearthly, unholy beauty. He was so transfixed by what he saw, he barely noticed what was happening to his own body. Though Alex had never been one for marathon sessions, only able to cum once before he lost the urge, his penis seemed to have a mind of its own.

It was odd, this unaccustomed feeling—troubling. Unconsciously, his hand moved down to caress his dick slightly. It throbbed anew. Alex experienced a flash of sadness and regret. In the back of his mind, he knew the reason: not one of the thirteen exquisite dicks pointing down at him was stirring at all.

CHAPTER 2

"Corey and I finally finished moving me into the condo. It wasn't as rough a job as I thought it was going to be. Thank God for that interior decorator—the one that gave Corey the truck. If we'd had to rent one..."

Alex knew he was talking to himself. The words poured out of him as he described his activities of the past few days much as he and Tony used to share the details of their daily lives each evening over dinner. He knew Tony couldn't hear him—his voice echoed from the muted mint green walls of the room, a color intended to relax and soothe, he'd been told. As silly as it might have seemed to speak to someone who was not truly present, Alex felt no embarrassment. He couldn't remain silent, or simply sit wrapped in grief, and couldn't speak the words he really wanted to say—the words of his heart, the phrases of his loss.

"I told you I rented out the townhouse, right?" He tried to inject as much positive cheerfulness as he could. "I knew you wouldn't agree to it but, honey, it's way too big for one person. I kept wandering around from room to room, hoping you'd be in one, and feeling lost. Besides, Roberto's moving back to Haiti or the Dominican Republic or wherever he's from and you know how tough it is to hire a responsible maid nowadays. It's only for six months so, if things change...with you, I mean..."

He reached out one hand, wanting to stroke Tony's bare upper arm, not knowing whether he intended to comfort his lover—who couldn't feel anything anyway—or himself, but he stopped short, wanting to make contact but unable to force his fingers the final fraction of an inch.

"I wish you could see the place. You know it used to be

a library, right? It's got stone floors—real marble—and this amazing paneling going halfway up the walls like that room we both liked when we took that tour of Versailles. The upper part is all wallpaper and Corey thinks it should come out. It's not in too terrible condition but it's got this ghastly pattern of vines and leaves—very distracting when I'm trying to work. And the background color? Red with gold flocking, can you believe it? There are these huge windows, six or maybe eight feet. The light keeps coming through and reflecting off that god-awful wallpaper and screwing up my sense of color when I'm trying to paint."

He paused, knowing he was rambling and then, continued in a softer voice.

"Yeah. You'll be happy to know I'm finally painting again." He smiled wryly, as if at a private joke. "Gotta pay the bills, right?"

It had been a longstanding joke between them, how Alex worked constantly but only had to make two or three sales a year to surpass Tony's more regular income at the travel agency. Tony had been—*was*—a vice president. Though his job responsibilities had more to do with promoting the company to the gay markets, and little to do with selling packaged tours and the like, he and Alex had gotten their fair share of luxury vacations and ocean cruises at dirt-cheap prices.

Alex remembered the last one, scarcely six months ago and still crystal clear in his mind, to a half-dozen tiny ports in the Mediterranean, some of which Alex had never heard of. The two of them had spent long, lazy days lying out on deck chairs with the sun sparkling off the deep blue water, covered in coconut scented oil and slowly roasting until their skins practically glowed. Tony's naturally dark skin, indicative of his Southern Italian ancestors, drank in the sunlight and browned deep chestnut with only the lightest of sun screens. Alex, being fairer, always resented having to use a higher SPF and to lie out longer in order to achieve a matching result. It was worth it to see the heads of the other passengers turn whenever they came into the dining room, linked arm in arm, one dark and one light. The picture they presented in their tailored tuxedos during the cruise's Formal Night was nothing less than breathtaking. Proud of his handsome partner, Alex had lapped up the attention like he was starving for it. It was so much more rewarding than the endless fawning that pseudo-knowledgeable collectors lavished on him whenever he reluctantly agreed to put together a full exhibit for Nadine's gallery.

Sycophancy irritated him, both as an artist and as a person. Far too few self-proclaimed experts could see the beauty of what Alex hoped he had created with his oils and brushes. Even fewer had the perspicacity to really *look* at the paintings or to divine the purpose behind them. Alex had never painted just to smear oil upon canvass; he sought to instill each work with meaning, to make a point which could be communicated even more effectively via the beauty of his work.

Theories, of course, abounded—almost every visitor to Nadine's had one. Alex had learned quite early in his career to mask his impatience with their inane speculations in favor of simply nodding, smiling pleasantly and agreeing with the ridiculous theories. In situations where the person complimenting his work—or criticizing it, for that matter—propounded something so ridiculous that it could have only been put forward by someone who had spent his adult life living on an alien planet, Alex simply effected mild surprise and responded, "You know, I never thought of that. Perhaps you're right." Then he would turn up the wattage on his smile and comment, "I guess sometimes even the artist isn't fully aware of what he's doing. Thank you *so* much for pointing that out to me."

Certainly, Nadine was mollified by his more mature approach. In the early years of his success, when he would rant and rave, and had no bones about calling the more inane collectors idiots to their faces, she had often had to step in to save the sale, using the excuse of "artistic temperament" as justification for Alex's boorish behavior. Since then, life had intervened and taken the edge off. He supposed he'd become complacent and, as a result, more tolerant. How not? He had a career beyond his wildest expectations, more money flowing in than he knew what to do with, a circle of good acquaintances to spend time with, an amazingly devoted friend in Corey and, of course, Tony.

Alex didn't care what the doctors said. As far as he was concerned, Tony was still the most beautiful man he'd ever known. Even though his chest and arms were beginning to lose their definition and to atrophy, in his mind's eye Alex could still see the remnants of the stunning physique that had recently spotted him for bench presses in the gym or filled out a suit with admirable sensuality or, even better, sprawled next to him nude on their king-sized bed. With his eyes narrowed, Alex thought he might even be able to ascertain the last vestiges of the magnificent tan from their cruise peeping through the pallor. But upon reflection, he had to admit to himself it was just an errant beam of light bouncing off the scarlet roses he'd placed on the bedside table when he'd arrived today. Wishful thinking, no matter how fervent, was still as tenuous a thing as was hope.

"Well, honey," he whispered. "At least you don't need to stress any more about that extra eight pounds you put on from all that rich food on the cruise." But the morbid humor fell flat and, looking at his lover's sunken cheeks behind the respirator, he felt the sting of hot, salty water trickling down his own.

He snatched a tissue from a box on the little rolling metal table, blew his nose noisily and cleared his throat. When he felt he could go on without breaking down into a blubbering mess, he forced a smile and went on.

"Anyway, it's a penthouse. The real-estate agent told me it used to be the office of some muckety-muck trustee or someone way back in the days when offices were bigger than the cubicles they have now. I'm telling you, it's huge—close to three thousand square feet and the ceilings are immense. Big cathedral jobbers all outlined in gilt or ormolu. I forget what it's called but it's as gold as the flocking on the damned wallpaper. Even in the bathroom, the ceiling's gotta be ten, maybe twelve feet high. When I'm sitting on the john, I feel like I'm at the end of some kind of tunnel or like there's this golden column of light beaming down on me from some Martian space ship that's about to abduct me. But the best, honey, the best part…the thing that made me sign the papers practically on the spot…"

He hesitated. Alex wanted to share every detail of his new lodgings with Tony, even if he knew he was in a coma and couldn't respond. But something about the statues, some deep and intense way they'd penetrated to that same wellspring which was the source of his own creativity, made him pause, strangely reluctant.

He took a moment to examine his thoughts. Weirdly, he felt his visceral reaction to the thirteen men on pedestals gracing the upper reaches of his new condo was more akin to unfaithfulness than his brief roll in the hay—or roll on the marble, as it were—with Corey had been. He'd never kept Tony in the dark about his occasional dalliances with Corey and, he surmised, Tony never really considered them marks of infidelity. He seemed to take them in stride as some kind of persisting immaturity on Alex's part. So long as the dalliances never assumed more serious import, and so long as there was never any danger of interference with their partnership, he was patiently accepting.

Not that Tony was any saint. Alex felt a brief flash of anger, much too intense for the thought, and almost instantly admitted to himself that his rage had more to do with Tony's present physical condition than any indiscretions he might have participated in during the course of their relationship. There had been more than a few such incidents over the years, mostly lasting only for a brief few minutes each in the sauna at the gym or, once in a while, an hour or three at some young man's conveniently located apartment. Alex had never felt threatened except once, several years ago, but the actor in question had gotten a decent role in a movie shooting abroad and had returned with a charming French boy in tow. In the aftermath, they'd even gone out to dinner a few times—two same-sex couples sipping expensive burgundy and chatting about nothing important. It had all been far too civilized but over time, they'd lost touch and Alex had no idea where to reach them to tell them about Tony's condition, and no clue if they were still together.

"There are these…things," he began slowly, fighting his reluctance to share. "They're statues, actually. I suppose you might even call them gargoyles of a sort."

Once again, he could see them, their smooth marble flesh suffused with the last vestiges of the light from the setting sun pouring through the windows. Oh, if only they were real. If only he could parade them through this sterile room with its metal-framed uncomfortable chairs and its banks of stale laminated cabinets and dull silver-fronted drawers. If only he could bring them here for Tony to see with his own delighted eyes, to banish the annoying hiss of the respirator and the incessant mechanical beeps of the monitors. To bring vibrant, wonderful *life* into this terrible place of misery and death.

How he'd love to watch Tony's reaction to the Zodiac Men. It would be like their own personal porn film set—not that they'd ever needed DVDs of other men having sex to inspire them. They would lay naked, holding each other in bed while the thirteen magnificent otherworldly bodies stood around them, watching and envying them, willing to trade their own beauty to experience the smallest measure of the passion the two human lovers shared for each other. Tony and Alex, secure in their love, grateful for the gifts they'd been given, would be magnanimous. One by one—or perhaps, two by two even!— they would invite these ethereal beauties to share in their lovemaking.

Sweet, innocent Virgo would be first, Alex thought, and they would go slowly, gently stroking his youthful figure with tender caresses, marveling that such a perfect creature could exist. Smooth-bodied, with round, almost androgynously slim muscles not quite fixed in their final form. Clearly no longer a boy, but not yet showing the first signs of roughness or hardening to his body to indicate he was in the full bloom of manhood. Practically hairless except for a light dusting of down where it counted, his dick rising slim and straight from a wispy thatch that was like soft pine needles that crowned plump, walnut-sized balls.

They would tease him, teach him, delight with him as his body experienced new sensations, drinking in each of his gasps of surprised pleasure as if it were the headiest of wines. They would lavish him with kisses, starting at his feet and tickling his toes with their tongues, moving upwards past the bulge of his calves and along his lean runner's thighs, avoiding his groin to heighten the anticipation. Wide-eyed with wonder at what was being done to him, he would eagerly accede to their rhythm, urging them to increase the tempo as he absorbed each sensation.

The boy would tremble, even more excited by being watched by his fellows than he was by the delicious shivers running through him. Discovering his own latent exhibitionism, he would angle his body, sweat-slicked and pulsing with the joy of his sexual initiation, to be better seen by the other twelve. Alex and Tony would each take one of his arms and, pinioning them over his head as he lay back on the bed so he could not push them away when the ecstasy became too much to bear, they would draw their tongues down his arms, from wrists to armpits, one on either side, licking and nibbling.

He would be shown, this pristine and innocent youth, the sensual delights of the body other than his cock and balls. His feet, the backs of his knees, the long expanse of his sides where the ribs were only thinly sheathed with supple muscle—all would be lavished with attention. They'd kiss the sleek column of his neck and nuzzle the hollow of his throat, pausing only to bestow kisses on his mouth, half-parted in anticipation, and upon one another's, breathing in his breath as if it were their own, tasting him and savoring the flavor, sweet and heady, like just-churned butter or recently mown grass. They would tease his taut little nipples, licking the tiny tight buds with simultaneous tongues, showing him women were not the only ones who could experience exquisite pleasure by attentions to the breast.

And when he was begging, even sobbing perhaps, that he could stand no more, Alex and Tony would gently roll dear, cherished Virgo onto his stomach. In front of all onlookers and with loving care, they would slowly introduce him to other pleasures. They'd use their fingers at first, rubbing lightly around the rosebud of his ass, brushing just their fingernails against the opening. Then, their mouths and tongues would come into play, taking turns, one of them teasing his hole while the other massaged and caressed his shoulders and back to reassure him. Cocks would be next, just the tips, probing but not penetrating—not yet—accustoming him to the feeling, priming his hole to gape and pucker, eager to receive what Alex and Tony were all too willing to give.

Tony would go first. Alex would gladly give him the honor of piercing the previously pristine territory of the boy's innermost being. Besides, if their pose in stone was any indication, Alex knew the Gemini would by this time already be engaged in a performance of their own for him to watch.

Virgo might cry out when Tony's huge dick pushed past the reflexive resistance. He would grab the pillow in slender fingers, clutching at it and biting down upon it to keep from voicing the sharp pain as he welcomed Tony inside. Within moments, passion would overtake the brief, sweet agony and he would respond, clenching and unclenching his newly plumbed butt muscles, urging Tony deeper, ever deeper, until the moment arrived when the end of Tony's cock touched that exquisite spot. Virgo would scream with joy, not pain, and his face would be suffused with a rapture of discovery at how incredible he felt. His body would shudder and thrash, and too soon it would be over, and Tony would withdraw, taking tender care.

The boy would collapse exhausted, imagining he could never again handle such a delicious assault. But Alex would be standing by, awaiting his turn. Virgo would roll onto his back, smiling up at Alex kneeling above him, sadly, as if to apologize that he had nothing left to give. Alex, however, knew better.

With Virgo splayed before him, he would lean down, licking the drops of cum from the end of the boy's dick with torturous patience, gradually bringing his lips into play. His tongue would lap the sides of the shaft, darting to tantalize the sensitive spot underneath where the shaft met the head. Virgo would feel his dick hardening, amazed it was capable of such a miracle so shortly after he'd thought it could never rise again. Alex would begin to work in earnest, swallowing the shaft so completely he could feel the wispy softness of the youth's pubic hair tickling his nostrils. Then he would retreat, almost freeing the dick entirely—but not quite. He would allow his lips to stay wrapped around the very end, his tongue flicking the opening to elicit maddening results. His head would surge forward quickly and then the withdrawal, agonizingly slow, again and again until Virgo could scarcely breathe.

The boy's fingers would scrabble wildly at the sheets as if seeking purchase to escape, but his body would betray him. His hips would buck forward to meet each of Alex's downward motions, the timing perfect. Tony would smile knowingly, having many times been on the receiving end of Alex's skills himself. And then, just when Virgo could stand no more, Alex would take pity upon him and…

"Sir?"

"Huh?"

Alex was abruptly jolted out of his fantasy. An older woman in a white skirt and blouse stood in the room, her silvery hair tucked neatly under her cap with only a wisp or two escaping, looking at him with an expression made up of two parts concern and one part embarrassment.

"Are you all right? We could hear you moaning from the nurses' station."

"Uh… I'm fine. Really."

Alex locked gazes with the woman, praying it would be enough to keep her from glancing down to where he could feel a hot stickiness spreading across the front of his shorts. Without looking away from her, he reached to the tray table and snatched up an abandoned magazine, whipping it onto his lap to conceal the stain. He hoped she hadn't noticed anything, but from the redness of her cheeks, he rather doubted it.

"If you're certain?" Fortunately, her tone was nothing but professional. Otherwise, Alex felt he might have just sunk into the linoleum floor from shame.

"Just…I mean… sometimes, it's hard to…." He grimaced at his poor choice of words and then motioned with his free hand to where Tony lay insensate; the other hand was occupied with making sure the magazine didn't slip. "It's a lot to deal with and sometimes…"

"I understand," she assured him, warm and kindly. But was that just a hint of a sparkle in her eye as if to say, "I know what you just did, you naughty, *naughty* boy"?

"Tragic. So tragic for such a handsome young man." She shook her head and sighed. "We didn't want to disturb you… interrupt your time together but…" The nurse tapped her wristwatch with one unpainted fingernail. "The shift change started ten minutes ago and…"

"Oh! Of course." Alex rose, careful to clutch the magazine firmly in place, and hobbled to Tony's bedside.

"There's still hope, you know," she said. "There's no effective treatment, as I'm sure the doctor told you. But sometimes patients just come out of it with no warning at all."

"I know. No warning at all. Just like when he took sick."

She lingered in the doorway for a moment. "I can give you a minute to say goodbye. To finish up whatever you were telling him, okay? I know what the doctors say, but," she lowered her voice conspiratorially, "I've always thought they could hear. Every word." Then she was gone.

"It's not important, sweetheart," he whispered when he bent down to kiss Tony's cool, still forehead. "I'll just save it for tomorrow. So you have something to look forward to."

A few moments later, Alex had reached the parking lot and was rummaging through his gym bag for a spare pair of shorts. While he was waiting for a family of five to pull out of their space so he could duck behind the car to change out of his soiled clothing, he had time to think.

He'd wanted to tell Tony about the Zodiac Men; in fact, he'd been looking forward to it. He'd thought he might have actually started in before he was…distracted, but he couldn't remember. Keeping Tony apprised of the little details of his day was one of the things that made it easier for Alex to cope with the disaster that had invaded their lives. He should have felt cheated of the opportunity.

Why then, this guilty feeling of relief?

CHAPTER 3

"It's about time, is all I can say!"

Alex winced. During the fifteen years he'd known the older woman, he'd never grown accustomed to Nadine's bray. At the beginning of every conversation, he had to stifle the urge to clap his hands to his ears to shield his eardrums so his hearing could adjust to the volume. The gallery owner-cum-agent claimed she'd become hard of hearing in her early sixties, thus the reason she tended to shout when she spoke. Alex suspected it was only an excuse. Hard-bitten, abrasive, and with a killer instinct for a profit, Nadine, he suspected, simply enjoyed yelling at people.

Not that she didn't care about Alex, perhaps even love him in her way. Nadine Shermer had certainly taken him under her wing when he'd first started painting, nurturing him and providing helpful criticism when he'd started meandering down paths she felt unworthy of him as an artist. She had convinced him not to undersell his own talent. But hers was a brand of tough love that Alex sometimes found hard to take. He knew she meant well, but the stress she invariably inserted into the time they spent together often left his nerves all jangled and raw; he always felt like a schoolboy who had been called into the principal's office for punishment.

Tony, on the other hand, knew how to handle her. She pretended to be annoyed by his shameless flirting but it was obvious to anyone who knew her more than casually that she was flattered by the attention. He could coax and wheedle her into docility in no time; she seemed to soften the moment he walked into the room. If Alex and Tony were, as she sometimes claimed, the kids she never had, Tony was undoubtedly her favorite child.

"Not your usual stuff, I see."

Nadine's eyes narrowed while she carefully inspected the painting, taking her time, absorbing each image and every stroke of the brush. She wore her usual frown—if she won the lottery, Alex doubted her expression would change—and it was impossible to tell if she liked the piece or not.

"Were you trying for some kind of symbolism?" she asked. "Or just experimenting?"

Wisely, Alex didn't respond, knowing she was talking more for the sake of working through her mental processes and not to garner an answer.

"Or maybe working out some inner demons?"

One eyebrow arched knowingly and she glanced at him to see if her comment elicited a reaction. Alex kept his expression carefully neutral.

The piece in question depicted the grotto of a classic English garden maze. Tall bramble hedgerows draped with vines of trailing flowers filled most of the canvas. Unkempt and ill-tended, it was obvious the place had been abandoned long ago and left to grow wild. In the center, a moss- and algae-covered fountain, its basin cracked and worn, stood waterless and empty, surrounded by a chipped granite bench and a few toppled and broken stone vases.

Alex was largely an Impressionist and even in this realistic scene, the work evidenced his style. Most of the age of the place was suggested by color rather than carefully structured details. The stones of the fountain and bench were bleary-edged with ochre and umber, the moss painted with greenish-gray brush strokes; even the abundantly wild flowering vines were muted, darker versions of their natural colors. The main tone of the work was somber, yet peaceful, but there was a slight overtone of something dark and troubling, mostly due to the choices of color.

Breaking through a gap in the hedge at one side was a young man, naked from the waist up, his fine, almost effete musculature suggested by the paint. Brown and maroon marred the creamy beige of his skin, suggesting he had been scratched by thorns and branches while fighting his way through the thicket. Alex had somehow managed to capture two conflicting emotions within the figure. There was a penumbra of vague fear, overlaid with a sense of relief. It was clear the young man had been lost for some time, had become terrified and panicked, and was grateful to have stumbled into the open space.

On the other side of the canvas, deeply shadowed, stood another man. He was somewhat older, perhaps in his thirties. Naked, his genitals masked by a clump of vine, he seemed only to have partly emerged from the dense foliage; perhaps some of his body had originated from it, as it was unclear where the vegetation left off and the human flesh began. Obviously, the boy was unaware of the other's presence, but a feeling of peace and safety emanating from the mysterious figure pervaded the painting and evidently was having its effect upon the youth. An observer could not help getting the impression that the boy would be saved.

"Amazing," Nadine finally breathed. "I don't think I've ever seen anything quite like it from you before. Couldn't resist the nudity, though, could you?"

Alex's propensity to paint exclusively male figures with at least one figure in each painting without clothing had been a bone of contention between them for years. Nadine believed he was limiting his audience. Alex felt he needed to paint what he knew, what most intrigued and fascinated him. Fortunately, at least so far, the buying public had tended to agree with Alex.

"Couldn't content yourself with a nice still life, huh? A basket of apples and a bowl of goldfish?"

Nadine grinned, something rare for her, and Alex correctly interpreted it as her really, *really* liking the piece. Hesitantly, he grinned back.

But suddenly, Nadine was all brittle business. "How soon can we expect more?"

"More?"

Nadine looked at him like he had rocks in his head. "I'll want twelve…no, make it fifteen. I'll talk to your publicist about it. Sean can come up with something. I'm thinking maybe we can promote it as an entirely new thing for you. Picasso had his Blue period, right?"

"Nadine, I'm hardly Picasso!"

"True. You're too close to realism."

"I meant…"

"I know what you meant," she snapped. "How many times do I have to warn you not to sell yourself short? Do you know how many artists would kill to be in your position? To get the prices you command? Kiddo, you've got to stop thinking of yourself as a dabbler and come to terms with the reality that you are a major artistic voice in contemporary impressionism."

It was an old argument with her, and one Alex didn't fancy having again.

"No one, I'm telling you," she said, "no one had the courage to work backwards like you did. Before Alex Restin came along, the Impressionists—well, the decent ones anyway—would have had heart attacks at the way you inject elements of strict realism into your work. This flower here…"

Her finger hovered over a single sprig of morning glory which Alex had rendered in exquisite detail, bursting in crystal clarity from those of its fellows rendered in a more abstract style.

"Or the line of the boy's forearm and hand. What is that he's holding? A map?"

Alex shrugged. He had no idea what he'd intended the torn piece of parchment to be. He knew only that while he was working, something inside him was adamant it had to be there.

"The rubble from this broken vase on the ground. The way you can see the bits and pieces from it scattered in the weeds." She shook her head. "The thing about a Restin, kiddo, is the remarkable way you include elements of strict realism that somehow heightens the whole Impressionist thing in the rest of the work. Lord save me from amateur painters who do the crappy things with the faces and hands coming out of the clouds and such! You do it with these tiny details that seem to make no sense why you chose 'em, and yet somehow they do."

She rubbed her hands together eagerly. "I'm gonna list it in the mid-six figures and see how it goes. Standard commission for the gallery. I promised Wannamaker dibs on anything I felt was truly spectacular, so if he wants it, I may cut him a little break. You okay with that?"

She didn't wait for a response before motioning one of her assistants to take the painting into the back room to prepare it for exhibition.

"You have any thoughts on the frame?"

"Something really simple," Alex suggested. "Or super ornate. D'you still have the one with all the vines worked into the wood? Might be a nice set-off for the garden theme. Just nothing halfway. I think it's gotta be full throttle one way or the other."

Nadine nodded, her eyes lingering on the canvas as it was carried away.

"So, March? April, maybe right after Easter? Or should we wait a month so they all get their tax refunds and are eager to spend 'em?"

"Huh?"

She was losing patience with his obtuseness. "For the showing, Alex. For the showing. Fifteen? Maybe a half-dozen in the new style? Most of them should be your tried-and-true, but try to inject some small elements of what's to come so the critics have something to write about. Progression of style, artistic maturity and all that crap. They just love to be able to impress themselves with the notion that they saw what was coming before the artist did himself. And, maybe you might do *one* without the pee-pees and butts?"

"There are no pee-pees or butts in this one." Alex said.

"Don't get your nylons in an uproar. I'm just saying, do you *know* how much we could get for an Alex Restin without even partial nudity? I'm talking shirts here, kid."

"It's not what I do. How much more than six figures could you possibly need? You can't spend the money you already have." As far as Alex was concerned, the matter was closed.

"Painters!" Nadine threw up her hands in disgust, but from knowing her as long as he had, Alex could tell she was doing it more for the dramatic effect than out of any real pique.

"You want tea?"

Alex grinned weakly. The offer of tea indicated Nadine was finished with the business aspects of their relationship and was about to launch into her preferred profession of trying to micromanage his personal life.

"Only if you have something other than that herbal crap you drink."

"Very *expensive* herbal crap," she corrected. "Come on back to the office and we can put our feet up and shmooze."

For the next five minutes or so, she busied herself running distilled water through the coffee maker and rummaging through one of the cabinets along the office wall and pulling out boxes of tea. Alex insisted on smelling each one until he found a blend less revolting than the ones Nadine preferred. He expected tea to taste like tea and not like someone had just boiled the trimmings from mowing a lawn.

"You go to see Tony today?" she asked once they were settled with their mugs. She pushed a tray of Danish butter cookies across the desk, indicating he should take one, but her question made any appetite he might have had flee.

"Last night."

She looked at him expectantly and he sighed. "No change, Nadine. The doctors tell me it could go on like this for a while. He'll either start to come out of it or..."

She shook her head. "How does a healthy young guy like Tony end up completely paralyzed in less than a week, I ask you? Something's not right with that." She leaned forward and pointed one arthritic finger at Alex's chest. "You tell those damned doctors that Nadine said so, you hear? With all the advances in modern medicine, you'd think those quacks could give him an injection or a pill or something..."

It was a familiar tirade and, as usual, Alex's soul winced at every word.

"It's some kind of new, mutated virus, Nadine. The regular kind always attacks healthy young men and no one knows why. They think it's a variant of whatever that guy who wrote *Slaughterhouse Five* had. Vonnegut."

"I don't read," came Nadine's flat reply. "Except the trade journals."

"They don't even have an actual name for it. They call it acute inflammatory polyneuropathy." He'd long since memorized the technical term, and though the doctors had explained it to him dozens of times, he still had trouble understanding what it meant, and even more difficulty applying all the ramifications of the disease to Tony's condition. "But they're always warning me that they're not sure. Guess they're worried about getting sued, huh?" He grinned weakly. "Bottom line is they don't quite know what Tony has."

"They got medicines for AIDS," she shot back. "Why not this?"

Alex shrugged tiredly. "Not enough money for research? Not enough people get it? They just discovered it? Damned if I know. We have to keep his body going artificially and see if he comes out of it."

"Just like that?" She snapped her fingers sarcastically, clearly meaning she thought the notion was ludicrous.

"Just like that. Joey Caprese took charge, since he and Tony go way back. He thinks that's the way it'll work. The Vonnegut disease—the one they already know about—comes on without much warning and leaves the same way. Joey's hoping this thing follows the same path. Two weeks from now, another six months, two years from now. Nobody can predict when. The longer it takes, the longer he'll have to be in therapy learning how to walk and stuff, learning how to breathe again."

"You up for that?" She was concerned, but as a mark of the depth of her affection for Tony, there was also a note of her daring him to say he wasn't. "Hospital beds in the house? Nurses around all the time? Strangers coming and going in white lab coats? Cleaning up after him when he can't use a bedpan?"

"I don't know." Alex was quietly miserable. "I just don't know. But I *do* know I'm gonna try."

She patted his knee. "That's all anyone can ask, kiddo. You know I'll help however I can."

Alex didn't doubt it. If the virus could be personified and made human-sized, he'd bet every last tube of paint that Nadine could harangue and bully it into submission. She shifted uncomfortably in her chair and studiously avoided meeting his eyes with her next question.

"What's the risk that when he comes out of it, he'll be…? I mean, he's in a coma, right? What about brain damage?"

"It's an *induced* coma," he corrected. "Not the normal way

they treat this, but because he's got this weird type, they thought putting him out completely would be best. Brain damage?" He spread his hands to show how helpless he felt. "Again, I just don't know."

"Work, Alex. Work will keep you sane, stop you from falling apart. Help you get rid of some of the…" She pounded one fist against her own chest, lacking adequate words to show what she meant. "It's not the money. Hell, you're right. Neither of us does this because we need more money. We do it for love. I do what I do because I'm crazy for talent—makes me positively wet. You do it because you're driven. I keep telling you all the great ones are, kiddo. So if it helps you to cope, I'll just bite my tongue and sell 'em. Even with the pee-pees and butts."

"I appreciate it."

"Soo…" She seemed to hesitate, then typically barged right in. "How are you handling…you know? Six months is a long time to go without."

Ten over-lacquered fingernails fluttered on her thighs on either side of her crotch.

"Nadine!"

"Don't jump down my throat. It's a healthy, normal question." Her jaw thrust out, belligerent and defensive. "You're a virile young man, Alex. You have needs. Hell, no one knows better than me how you used to fill those needs before Tony came along—or how often. You're an artist; you need human contact. Rosy Palm and her five friends are not gonna cut it for you."

"Jesus, Nadine." Alex was more flustered than he could remember being in a long time. "I'm not comfortable discussing this with someone old enough to be my mother."

"More like your grandmother," she said, grinning. "Seriously, what are you doing for extracurricular? You talk to your therapist about it? I'll bet you she agrees with me, doesn't she?"

Reluctantly, Alex nodded. Nadine continued her interrogation relentlessly.

"Corey helping out?"

"Once," Alex confessed, blushing. "But mostly, I'm not in the mood. No drive. Not with Tony…"

"This is about you, not Tony. Tony's not missing anything at the moment."

"Well," he began, hesitantly. "There are these guys..."

"Guys? As in guy plural?" Now it was Nadine's turn to be shocked.

"Thirteen of them, actually." Alex was quite enjoying her discomfort as her penciled-in eyebrows rose a good inch.

"Thirteen?"

Oddly, it wasn't as difficult as he'd feared it would be to discuss the Zodiac Men. Perhaps it was because of the almost familial relationship he had with Nadine. Or perhaps it was because she was female.

"They're stunningly beautiful. All of them. They're living with me, in fact."

He thought the gallery owner might choke on her tea.

"You're putting me on, right?"

"No," Alex began, and then decided to save her from the stroke it looked like she was about to have. "And yes."

He drew the pause out as long as he could, luxuriating in her expectant silence. When Nadine wanted information, it was rare she kept quiet and waited for an answer. Usually she bullied and shouted until she got it.

"The new condo is on the top corner of a building that used to be a library," he began, once he'd organized his thoughts and decided how he felt most comfortable describing the statues.

"Yeah, yeah. I know that."

"The main living part is a huge round room with a sort of cupola on top, or a belfry kind of thing. It has a skylight on one side and gigantic windows starting about seven feet from the floor and going up to the bottom of the dome. Between them, are twelve pedestals with..." His memory roved over the details of the men and, wiser after his incident in the ICU, he made sure he held the large mug of tea Nadine had given him was in a strategic position, blocking her view of his crotch.

"With...?" she prompted.

"Art."

"Art?" From her tone, it was clear Nadine had expected a racier response. "Sculpture, I'm assuming?" She rarely dealt in anything other than paintings and had occasionally offended bothersome sculptors by referring to them as "chipper shredders."

"Like you've never seen."

Alex leaned forward in his chair. He didn't know why he'd been so affected by the statues' presence, but if anyone could understand how deeply he'd been touched by their beauty, it would be Nadine. Yet somehow he found himself reluctant at the thought of inviting her over to examine them for herself. It was almost as if to allow someone who was not as young, as beautiful, and as male as they were would somehow sully and cheapen Alex's experience. He needed to satisfy her curiosity but not make her want to actually see them.

"The Zodiac. I guess you could call them gargoyles because they're not all entirely human. Life-sized and incredibly beautiful. Let's see…Pisces is a merman and Sagittarius, of course, is a centaur."

"I'm Scorpio," Nadine told him unnecessarily. God help any of her artists who forgot to make a big deal out of her birthday each November.

"Tattoos," Alex said dreamily. "A guy maybe my age. Great shape like a gymnast. Covered with these amazing carved tattoos. I haven't had time to go out and buy a ladder yet so I can get up there and see 'em up close but, the one in the center of his chest is big enough to make out from the floor. It's a scorpion. And the claws…" Alex held his hands to his own chest to demonstrate. "The claws sort of pinch at each nipple and the tail and the stinger kind of rise up to his throat."

"Ouch. Sorry I asked." Nadine crossed her hands on her breast like she was protecting them and made an exaggerated grimace. "My ex-husband was Cancer."

"Armor. One of those shoulder-plate things on one side. The other has a—what would you call it?—a greave? running up the biceps. His thighs are encased in something similar and, I think, he's got a sword in one hand." Alex couldn't help his flush of arousal at the thought of the metaphoric sword, clearly visible through the sculpted fine mesh of a chain mail loin cloth, that Cancer gripped tightly in his other unencumbered hand.

"I've never seen anything like them," he added. "Though the sculptor was working in the classical style, with all the detail on the dicks and the homo-eroticism, they strike me as being remarkably contemporary work. I checked with the real-estate agent and he can't find out anything about their origins. The library records were stored in the basement and lost in a fire just before the condo conversion. I'm hoping there's some kind of artist's mark on the bases. Gotta remind myself to pick up that ladder."

"*This* is your sex life?" Again, it was clear she was more than a little worried about his mental state. "I've heard of wanting a stiffie before, but this is ridiculous."

"It's better than renting porn." Alex shrugged. "There's this amazing vibrancy about them. It's almost like they are a second away from coming down off the wall and…well, in my…er…fantasies, they do."

"Hire a hooker." The advice came in a no-nonsense, practical tone.

"Not my style."

"Take advantage of Corey, then."

Alex grinned. "Much as I love him, a little Corey goes a long way."

"Yeah, about ten inches if I read the bathroom walls right."

"Nadine!"

"Sorry." She didn't even have the decency to look embarrassed. "I always distrusted guys who feel they need to stuff socks down the front of their pants."

"Trust me. It's real. No socks."

"Stop," she said, deadpan. "You're gonna give me a hot flash." She paused to take a sip of now tepid tea and made a face at the lack of heat. "Seriously, kiddo. I'm not advising an affair or anything. I *know* Tony's gonna be fine, just fine. But, in the meantime, you've gotta do something to release all that pent-up…stuff. If not for your sanity, then do it for the sake of the art. You know you don't work so well when you're not getting it on a regular basis. Jeez, I remember those three pieces you did when the two of you were on your little honeymoon. I still think they're some of the best things you ever painted."

"I'm fine." Alex stood up to leave. All this talk about the stone men made him eager to get back to them. "Don't worry about me. I've got my gargoyles and my imagination." He grinned. "That's more than enough for anyone, right?"

The sun had long passed the point where the northern light, so highly prized by most painters, had ceased to illuminate the condo. For Alex, this was not the disadvantage it would at first seem; his paintings had always been created with the idea that they would be best viewed in a muted, indirect light to heighten their dream-like quality. It was one of the many innovations Alex Restin was known for.

Boxes and small crates still littered the huge expanse of the main living area, which also contained Alex and Tony's bed, carefully placed directly under the center skylight. Alex hoped that once Tony recovered and could be brought home, they would be able to spend long, sultry nights making love under the tender gaze of stars through the paneled glass panes. It was something he longed for but, over the past few days, had begun to doubt would ever happen. The real-estate agent had assumed Alex would use the deep recessed alcove located off the living room as their bedroom, but instead, Alex had decided it should be reserved as Tony's home office. Besides, the master bathroom had been installed on the other side of the open central space and was much more conveniently located to the area under the skylight. What would eventually be the office was next to what Alex thought might have once been a wet bar. There was a sink, cabinets and a large mirror, but no toilet, bath or shower and, from the center of the living room, it was fully exposed.

He and Corey had quit unpacking around dusk. They'd managed to manhandle most of the furniture into its ultimate location, except for Tony's desk, computer and file cabinets, which were still stacked in their cartons in the alcove. The kitchen area—also open to the living room—still needed work, but at least the dining table and chairs had been set up. They'd filled the wardrobe and dresser drawers with Alex's and Tony's clothes all mingled together, and so long as they were temporarily out of sight, Alex would deal with sorting them out later. Their possessions that were not immediately essential remained in boxes organized by content on the many shelves which lined three of the curved walls and presumably had once held rare library books.

Alex's studio space had warranted most of his and Corey's efforts. He'd decided to install it directly across from the front door, near where the Gemini stood, with enough space between his workspace and the wall so that by simply raising his eyes and turning full circle, he could take in all of the statues without leaving his position in front of the easel.

Corey had left, though reluctantly, to meet his date for the evening. He'd made it quite clear he'd be willing to stay if Alex was amenable to a repeat of the other afternoon. But Alex had begged off with the excuse that he needed to work. Corey took the rejection gracefully but still managed to maneuver his tongue halfway down Alex's throat when they kissed goodbye while pressing his shirtless, sweating chest tightly up against Alex's front and groping his ass. Alex smiled at the memory. Corey was incorrigible—and predictable.

Now, Alex stood wearing nothing but his favorite pair of paint-stained shorts, with daubs of pigment smeared across his brow and cheeks from where he'd absently wiped away the perspiration with one of the rags he used to clean his brushes. His chest, arms and thighs looked like he'd been tortured by some Spanish Inquisitor who had a rainbow fetish, with sharp slashes of color running every which way. There was a particularly large splotch of white on his upper abdomen that materialized when, absorbed with the problem of getting the effect of the moonlight reflecting from the water just as he wanted it, he'd scratched a mild itch.

The painting he was working on was very much in his new style—hopefully, Nadine would be pleased. A young man stood on the shore of a rocky beach, his body angled partially away from the water. Typical of a Restin, he was almost nude, with only a few strands of seaweed draped over one shoulder. One of his finely muscled legs was exposed to the viewer, along with the suggestion of a sweep of perfect buttock. His other leg, as well as his genitals and one hip, were hidden—either because of the way the figure was positioned or by an almost waist-high outcropping of rock. Alex had chosen the seaweed and the vestiges of sand clinging to the youth's shoulder and upper back to lavish with detail, as well as a tiny crab that scuttled along the waterline in the foreground.

It was clear the youth was leaving the beach but was reaching back with one hand, his face turned to another man just emerging from the water. There was unutterable sorrow on his face—and longing, as if he were obligated to depart when there was nothing in the universe he would rather do than to remain. As for the man still halfway in the sea, his smile confirmed that when the youth returned, he would be welcomed.

Their arms reached for each other. Their fingers almost touched and the rocks in the landscape appearing in the background of the empty space between their groping hands sprang into focus in such realistic detail that individual tufts of marsh grass could be seen. The two men themselves were in soft focus, the details of their bodies obscured as if the light from the moon was blocked by a passing cloud.

The painting's ambiance was sorrow and longing and regret, yet there was a peaceful quality. Though time might pass between meetings, it was clear the lovers knew they would eventually be reunited.

The antique grandfather clock in the far corner of the condo struck midnight with rich, rounded bongs, startling Alex from his concentration. He glanced at it, not having realized it was so late, and grimaced when his view also took in the blink of the digital clock across the room on the bedside table. The move must have screwed up the works of the grandfather; it was actually past two in the morning.

Wiping his hands on a rag, getting more new paint on them than he managed to remove, he decided to call it a night. Rather than mess up the master bathroom, he threw down his rag, quickly cleaned his brushes in the old coffee cans he saved for just that purpose, and crossed to the former wet bar to wash up. Sweat trickled down his back and, combined with the paint smears gracing the front of his torso, made him sticky. The condo had air conditioning, of course, but while he worked,

Alex left it off, believing it adversely affected the way the paint dried.

He still felt grungy and sweaty but he was tired from his long hours of concentration, so he didn't want to bother drying off after a shower—no matter how quickly—before tumbling into bed. Instead, he ducked his entire head under the faucet, closing his eyes so as not to get water in them, and blindly fumbled for a towel. Before he could lay his hands on one, he was aware of a sudden coolness pervading the room, something damp but not unpleasant, as if he'd left a window open on a rainy night. With a start, he sensed a presence behind him. Blinking to clear his vision, he was turning away from the sink to confront the intruder when he felt moist, cool hands gently grip his sweaty shoulders.

He stiffened in panic. The fingers stroked softly, easing the tension from his muscles, and able to open his eyes at last, Alex saw that the mirror over the sink reflected no one but himself. Frightened, he whirled around and stopped. His jaw dropped.

CHAPTER 4

The man before him was a paragon of physical perfection. Long and lean, with the body of a swimmer or diver, his chest was lightly muscled but the shoulders were broad and corded. His face was exotic, foreign, and he had a small but well-formed nose, with just a hint of the Asiatic in the almond-shaped eyes. Cool, long fingers rested on both Alex's shoulders and, unable to stop himself, Alex reached out to hold the intruder, resting his hands on either side of the man's naked waist.

Alex gasped at the contact. The man's skin, which appeared so smooth, so unmarred at a distance of less than a foot, was actually pebbled, as if by microscopic goose bumps. Alex could feel the tiny protrusions in the pads of his fingers and in the flesh of his palms, and there was a sleek oiliness to it, not unpleasant—strangely erotic, in fact—as if his hands could glide over the body of this exquisite creature for hours and feel no friction.

With his intake of startled breath, Alex took in the man's scent. Briny sea water and the tang of ocean vegetation, with the underlying smell of maritime breezes and a scintilla of the clean, fresh smell of just-caught fish which, Alex knew from childhood summers spent by the shore, was not at all fishy or pungent. Fascinated with the skin texture, Alex moved his hands lower, seeking to trace the line of the man's hips, or to move his palms around to cup the firm butt, which he somehow knew was as perfectly formed as the rest of him.

For an instant, Alex frowned at the change in what he felt. At first, his mind couldn't grasp the meaning of the rough yet slick surface sliding beneath his fingers. He glanced down, but even before anything registered, he already knew. From the waist down, there was almost nothing human.

The tail's scales were an intoxicating mix of cerulean blue and iridescent green, shot through with flakes of gold, each scale moist and glistening. Unlike the torso, it was bulging with muscle; it would have to be for this veritable god from the sea to balance so casually upon it. As Alex brought his eyes back upwards to focus on the dick, fully erect and thrusting proudly from the rounded triangle of human flesh that punctuated the creature's groin at the top of the tail, his artist's eye took in the faint greenish hue of his skin, an odd but weirdly attractive color, so subtle he'd at first failed to notice it.

Pisces leaned forward and stopped, his lips poised so close to Alex's that the artist could practically taste the salty tang of his breath. It evoked raw clams, dug from the beach at twilight and slipped onto the tongue and down the throat with nothing but seawater as garnish, and the buttery sweet taste of crab, sucked from the claw with gluttonous abandon. Alex could practically hear the distant, high-pitched, piercing cry of sea gulls roosting on flotsam out on the open sea and smell tendrils of seaweed washed up on the beach at night, a scent reminiscent of a vast, open vista stretching like the ocean onwards toward forever, punctuated only by the soothing rumble of waves rolling into the shore.

The flavor, when their tongues met, was everything it had promised to be and ever so much more.

Alex's right hand moved from the creature's ass to grasp the back of his head, urging him forward, ever forward, while Alex desperately probed deeper with his tongue to devour the salty essence, savoring the taste of him. He felt the puckered clumps of seaweed tangled in Pisces' hair, hard rubbery nodules that were a larger version of the bumps on the slick, cool skin of his torso. His other hand slid from Pisces's waist, fingertips brushing at the sharp edges of scales before the surface changed and Alex was able to experience the more-human wonder of the taut-muscled ass. Alex gripped it tightly, pulling his otherworldly lover's groin closer into his own, letting up only when he felt feathery wisps of something trailing dangling from the small of Pisces's back and ticking the backs of his hands. Curious and with some reluctance, he halted his exploration of the fish-man's butt and moved upwards to encounter clusters of tiny shells—cockles maybe—trapped in a silky webbing of mossy tendrils, still moist from the sea.

The pulsing of the mollusks as they opened and closed their shells, hunting for oxygen, penetrated Alex's sensitive fingertips, traveling up his arms and across his chest. He felt his breath and heartbeat alter to match their rhythm, and when at last all was in sync, he knew the inner peace of the seas, the comfort of a liquid womb which he had not experienced since just before birth.

He broke the lip lock and stepped back, coming up short against the sink, wanting to take in every detail of this strange and exquisite creature. But Pisces seemed to have another idea in mind and would not be denied. He gently took hold of Alex's hand and with a firm tug drew him forward across the room until they were standing atop one of the canvas tarps Alex had spread out earlier to protect the marble floors from errant drops of paint. With inexorable force—not violent but so strong Alex could do nothing but give in to it—Pisces bore him to the floor. The artist lay on his back as the merman poised above him, a fold of canvas clinging to one shoulder with the tackiness of partly dried paint.

Pisces smiled down at him, a secret smile of anticipation, as if he was about to bestow a delightful and unexpected gift—as indeed he was. Alex reached up, wanting to pull the fish-man in for another kiss, but Pisces shook his head. Firm-muscled forearms with long, slim lengths of membranous flesh along the outside—fins, Alex thought—grasped his wrists and placed them firmly back at his sides. Alex remained still, waiting, feeling completely powerless. He felt he should have been frightened; instinctively, he knew he was about to be ravished, but he suspected it would be with excruciating tenderness. The throbbing pulse in his temples, the echo of the sea, calmed him.

Pisces's fingers rested on Alex's chest just below his collarbone, barely touching him. Alex longed to arch forward, to press his flesh into the pebbled pads of fingers, to feel their moist coolness against his hot and flushed skin, but Pisces seemed to sense the intended motion and, with another smile—this one mischievous—he shook his head.

Slowly, so slowly that Alex could scarcely bear it, the fingers moved inwards, meeting just below the hollow of his throat, and then moved down. Where they passed, the nerves beneath the artist's skin came alive as a thick, oily fluid oozed from the fish-man's fingers, penetrating the flesh and sparking the neurons beneath. For a moment, Alex wondered why he wasn't uncomfortable; being covered with some kind of alien slime was not an erotic experience he'd ever fantasized about, much less experienced. But the effect was that of some sense-heightening drug absorbed by his skin, and as Pisces continued to stroke and softly knead his torso, Alex found he had erotic zones where he'd never known it was possible to have them.

Inside Alex's shorts, his penis engorged and strained against the zipper, bulging with the most magnificent erection he'd ever had until he feared it would burst right through the cotton. He'd always had sensitive nipples—his "high points," Tony had called them—and anyone who teased the hair of his armpits was rewarded with Alex's moans. But who knew the skin along his ribs could experience such ecstasy? He'd never before thought he might cum merely from the touch of someone's hands tracing the lines of his upper stomach where his six-pack became an eight-pack. And when Pisces moved lower and began sweeping his fingers and palms along both the inside and outside of Alex's thighs, Alex began to fear he might pass out from the intensity of the sensual torment. Tingles shot through his calves, and seemed to bypass his groin to flush his chest and elicit gasps of pleasure before moving back down his torso and belly and shooting up through the shaft of his penis to home in on the tip of his dick. By the time the fish-man concentrated his efforts on the soles of his feet, fingers weaving between each toe with languorous teasing, Alex thought he might go mad.

The merman, with no legs or feet of his own, seemed fascinated by Alex's. He lavished attention on them until Alex—who'd never understood foot fetishes, much less had one of his own—involuntarily curled and uncurled his toes with heels drumming lightly at the floor, back arched, his hands clutching at the canvas as he cried out, begging Pisces to take pity upon him, to stop and grant him release. But Pisces seemed to possess a hint of harmless sadism, and instead he brought his mouth down to the big toe of Alex's right foot and enveloped it.

Alex screamed, an inarticulate sound of consummate pleasure, trying desperately to absorb the sensation. His hands released the canvas in favor of slapping at the floor—anything to divert himself from the delicious waves of erotic torment rippling up from his toes, past his ankles, along his thighs and onwards. One by one, each toe of both feet was suckled in turn and then—oh, the delicious agony of it!—the merman's tongue attacked the soles of his feet with long slow licks from heel to toes, each calculated to pierce any remaining reserve in the artist's body and reduce him to a quivering mass of raw and stimulated nerves.

When he seemed satisfied that he'd pushed Alex well past the point when any human could withstand the sensual overload, Pisces paused for a long moment, admiring his handiwork. The odd marine lubrication covered the entire front of Alex's body, except for the parts still concealed by the shorts. Leaning forward in a push-up position along the length of his helpless victim, Pisces lowered himself with tantalizing patience until the two men were pressed together chest to chest. For Alex, it was like an electrical current ran from the fish-man's skin directly into his own wherever their flesh made contact. Tiny waves ebbed and flowed against him, their throbbing establishing synchronicity with his dick. His hips bucked; he could not stop, thrusting upwards, seeking friction to allow release where no friction was to be had.

While Alex cried out, begging to be freed of the confining shorts, pleading with Pisces to allow him to stroke his hard, pulsing cock, the merman's hands and body were not idle. He wriggled his chest, trying to grind himself against Alex and succeeding only in depositing more of the gelatinous sensation-heightening slime, slipping and sliding atop him while his hands slid along the artist's arms. Finally, he grabbed onto the firm flesh of Alex's lats, holding him flat against the floor, and with strong, rippling, bunching and cording motions of his tail, began to pump his groin up and down against the shorts, slapping their stomachs together where they clung for an instant, only to be separated with a moist sucking sound.

A deep, guttural gasp built up in the back of Alex's throat—mindless and wordless yet unarguably the vocal emanation of a physical passion driven beyond the limits he could stand. It erupted in a harsh cry, primal and strong, and the instant he gave voice to it, his dick exploded, pumping his cum into his shorts like a tsunami. The thick milky semen soaked through the material almost instantly, its volume so great that a portion of it oozed past the waistband of the shorts to pool in his navel.

He shot for what seemed a very long time, his arms slapping the canvas, his feet thrashing against the marble. When his twitching dick had expelled the final droplets of sperm, his body shuddered and he collapsed backwards, lying with limbs akimbo, exhausted.

Alex didn't know how long he lay there, but when he finally found strength to open his eyes, Pisces was gone. Alex sat up to find the statute on its pedestal—from his supine position, he could look straight up at it—but his tantalizing lover of only moments before had vanished.

Wondering if it had all been some weird erotic daydream, Alex laboriously hauled himself to his feet. Though he could scarcely walk, he knew he had to drag himself into the shower or risk covering the bed with gunk. Under the steaming water, his nerves eventually settled and he blushed shamefully at the lengths to which his creative libido could go, spinning fantasies of such imagined realism. By the time he had dried himself and was wrapped in a fluffy towel and ready for bed, he had convinced himself the entire incident was caused by paint fumes. True, it was only acrylic, but he'd noticed earlier that the new condo had little ventilation and the mild toxins must have built up and affected his brain. He resolved to find a way to pry at least some of the windows open as soon as he had the chance.

When he tumbled into bed, knowing his sleep would be sweet, he had already chastised himself to curtail his overactive imagination in the future. Maybe Nadine was right and he should just bite the bullet—not that it would be any sacrifice to do so!—and look to Corey to take care of his needs while he waited for Tony's recovery. Alex's eyelids grew heavy; his breath evened out and soon he was blissfully unconscious. Tomorrow morning, he would look back on this as nothing but a delicious, if exhausting, exercise of his subconscious.

Deep in slumber, he was unable to witness the pale, milky green jelly smeared on the condo floor, slowly evaporating. By the time he awoke, like the merman, it would be gone.

"It's an unusual coping technique, I'll give you that. But hardly unexpected. You're a young man, and if you're not willing to take care of things, your body will do it for you. We both know you've never been a monk. Though I'd suggest if you're going to act out sexually, you might wanna try something more tantric."

For the fiftieth time since the session started, Alex wished Cheryl was a more traditional therapist and had put a couch in her office. He couldn't deny how much she'd helped him deal with Tony's situation during these past few months, but he always found it difficult to meet her eyes when he was confessing something intimate. He wasn't sure if it was some kind of natural reluctance inherent in the relationships between therapists and patients or if it was because he was uncomfortable talking about the details of his sex life—even if it *was* just fantasy—with a woman.

"In fact, if my memory hasn't failed me, before Tony, you could have given a major porn star a run for his money."

Alex blushed. The wanton activities of his younger days weren't so far in the past that he couldn't clearly remember them—and sometimes look back on them with a mild longing regret.

"Several porn stars." He couldn't resist the urge to try to shock her. "Three of 'em at a time at one of the White Parties."

Cheryl knew exactly what he was trying to do and refused to give him satisfaction by expressing even mild disapproval. She just continued in that same measured and dry tone that Alex mentally referred to as her Non-Judgmental Voice.

"My point exactly. Monogamy never felt natural to you, right?"

"Until Tony."

To Alex's surprise, Cheryl rolled her eyes. "You are *not* going to try to tell me you were faithful. Lying, even to yourself, does not sit well with the universe. What about Corey?"

"Corey doesn't count."

"And the three-way?"

Alex felt his lower jaw set stubbornly. "That was only twice. It didn't work the first time and after the second try, we *knew* it wasn't going to work. Dammit, Cheryl. My husband is in a coma, maybe even dying, and all you want to do is remind me of what a whore I was? What kind of therapy…?"

"I'm trying to remind you that whatever your feelings for Tony, he's not able to give you the release you need. I'm trying to tell you the guilt you're feeling is completely natural. You need to take that guilt and personify it. Think of it as something physical. Wrap it up in a mental box and take some time meditating on it. Commune with it. Seek to understand it and remove its power over you. Come on, Alex. Look at this logically. It's not like you've set up shop in a bathroom stall at the bathhouse. You had a couple of fantasies…" She held up her hand to quiet him when he began to object and tell her, yet again, how real they'd seemed. "Wet dreams. That's all they were, Alex. Wet dreams. Might do you some good to spend a couple of hours focusing on your erotic chakras."

"I never had a wet dream that real before," he muttered.

"You've never been under this kind of stress before either. Time's almost up but, here's something to think about for next week. I'll make you a bet, okay?"

"What kind of bet?" Alex didn't bother hiding his suspicion. Somehow, Cheryl always seemed to be right about things and it annoyed the shit out of him.

"I think you'll have at least one more of these incidents. What's more, now that you know part of what you're feeling is guilt— even though you refuse to admit it—I'll bet your subconscious will tap into that guilt. I think you may even start to punish yourself."

Alex laughed bitterly. "If you think I'm going to start dreaming about whips and chains, you'd better think again. That's never been my style."

"I don't think it'll be quite that obvious." God, how he wanted to wipe that smug, all-knowing smile off her face. "But mark my words, punishing yourself is next."

Alex had decided to call the newest painting *Reunion Delayed*, knowing it was a lousy title and that Nadine would probably change it. He finished applying the last few strokes of varnish and stood back to make sure the coat was even. Satisfied, he stepped away and allowed his gaze to drift upwards. Taking in the lush details of the statues one by one, lingering with fond memory and a little embarrassment on both Virgo and Pisces, he noticed that tonight the skylight was firmly propped open to allow the varnish fumes to escape. No matter what Cheryl had said, and no matter how delightful the illusion had been, Alex had resolved there would be no more sexual interludes with pieces of marble come to life.

Corey had called several times but Alex let the machine pick it up. The first time he didn't answer because he was up on a ladder, wrestling with a chisel to free the skylight from where it had been painted shut. From the playful tone in Corey's voice when he left the message, Alex knew *exactly* why his friend was calling and Alex simply didn't feel up to it. Besides, he'd been up until the wee hours the night before and he needed to get some sleep. Nadine had arranged a morning showing with Charles Wannamaker of the piece Alex had given her, and she expected him to be there. The older man had never been able to disguise his attraction to the blond artist and, Nadine felt, Alex's presence always loosened Wannamaker's wallet to the tune of an extra ten or fifteen grand.

Exhausted and a little high from the fumes in spite of the open skylight, Alex tumbled into bed and was fast asleep in minutes. The dreams, when they came, were nebulous things, full of white marble arms and legs intertwined with brief flashes of muscled torsos and tantalizing glimpses of erect stone cocks. Never able to get a clear view—and desperately wanting to—Alex tossed and turned in his sleep, restlessly striving to see, to *touch*, and always being denied. When he woke himself up a scant two hours later, he lay on his back in the darkened bedroom, bathed in sweat, frustrated and suffused with a strange sense of longing, his aching dick as hard as the proverbial rock.

He thought about the thirteen beautiful and unobtainable men standing over him. In a way, he supposed, they were keeping guard, watching him; he found a sense of comfort in the thought. For a long time he lay there, wondering if he would experience another visitation, but as the long moments dragged on, he was disappointed. Looking up, he could see flickers of heat lightening through the open skylight. He knew he should get out of bed and close it in case it rained, but he was too damned tired to move. Besides, the tingle in his dick was getting worse, distracting him and demanding attention.

Figuring he might as well take care of the problem himself, he brought his hand to his mouth and spit into his palm to provide lubrication. He rolled down the waistband of his boxers but, before he could grab his own cock, the darkness was split by a flash of lightening and the dull rumble of thunder. With a gasp of surprise, followed immediately by a sense of grateful anticipation, Alex felt his hand grabbed and forcibly moved away.

"Don't you people knock?" he mumbled, more to himself than to make his protest heard.

He sighed, his body already tingling at the sensations he imagined he was about to experience. His back arched, his hands reached up, eager to explore the naked body above him, intensely curious to know which of the statues it was. Alex was ready.

"Ouch!"

His wrists were seized roughly and his arms quickly pinioned above his head. He started to struggle but the weight descending on his chest almost knocked the wind out of him. His nostrils filled with a pungent smell like wet wool and he fought unsuccessfully against his captor's grip, his body thrashing and twisting to get out from underneath. Whichever of the Zodiac Men it was, he was immensely strong. Panic set in and Alex had just opened his mouth to cry for help when another lightning flash gave him a good look at his assailant.

He gasped at the animal beauty of his attacker. Fascinated

by the lightning somehow reflected by and captured in the creature's eyes, Alex saw the light slowly spread throughout its body.

First, the rough-hewn handsome features of the face were illuminated. Thick, craggy brows framed a broad nose sloping down to wide, puggish nostrils. Alex thought he was imagining the cloudy vapor trickling from the man's nose as he breathed, until he caught a whiff of it—like wet cloth left to dry in an open field of hay—and knew the steam was not just his mind playing tricks.

Alex gasped at the two huge striated spirals of rounded bone emerging from the man's temples, the horns twisting upon themselves in a glorious and unmistakable exhibition of primal maleness. The glow spread down the corded pylon of muscled neck and across an expanse of shoulders that seemed to go on forever. The massive chest was revealed with tantalizing languor, smooth and cool looking, just like the marble it had been carved from—and equally as hard, impressive evidence of raw, brutal strength. The pectorals rose from the breastbone where they were born in a ripple of muscle, the mounds swelling in a sheath of creamy pale skin as they built to an apex topped with nipples the size of eraser heads, surrounded with wide aureoles of darker flesh. When the upper torso was fully revealed by the creeping light, Alex noticed *this* body was never meticulously sculpted in a gym for looks only; its development was natural, honed from hard, strenuous work. The much-sought-after washboard stomach was absent, instead replaced with a single slab of striated muscle. In a decade or so, it could expand into the standard body-builder's paunch, but for now it was hard, so hard Alex thought that to punch it would be to injure his fist.

As his eyes drank in more, Alex was not surprised he had been so easily overpowered. The man would have been grotesquely over-muscled had his body not been so sleekly in aesthetic harmony with itself. There was a sublime perfection to him that Alex's artist's eye was quick to appreciate. He glanced down, and with a gasp saw the man's dangling balls revealed as the light reached them. They were practically the size of plums and his cock, still only semi-tumescent, and yet easily as thick as a soda can and twice as long, was a veritable caveman's club of a dick.

Alex wanted to surge forward and swallow it, to choke himself with the rapture of feeling such a staff probing at the back of his throat, to take each testicle into his mouth in turn—as he doubted he could fit them both at the same time—and suckle them until they were dripping with his saliva, but at his motion, the pressure on his wrists increased to a painful level and he could do nothing but lie there, trapped.

There was a grunt, and in the back of his mind Alex thought this might be the first of the Zodiac Men who had made any sound whatsoever other than the normal verbal gasps and groans during sex. This sound, however, was different. It was harsh and demanding and, unless Alex's ears deceived him, held a note of something that made him uncomfortable.

Alex knew who had come to ravage him.

Aries smiled when he saw the recognition in the artist's eyes, and the smile grew broader when he saw the dawning fright. For Alex instinctively knew his experience with the Ram, the personification of the God of War, would be no gentle exploration of lovemaking. No, it was obvious that Aries would take what he wanted, in any way he desired, and any cries of protest or yelps of pain would be ignored.

Aries leaned forward, and the plumes of mist shooting from his nose thickened as the beast's lust heightened. His tongue, when it thrust past Alex's lips, was large and rough, and Alex could not help thinking it was as thickly muscled as the rest of him. It probed roughly, choking Alex not just with its bulk, but by its scent and taste. The wet wool smell was undercut with something sharper, a tang which Alex oddly associated with both the open outdoors and with violence. His mind frantically traveled down the corridors of memory as he fought to breathe, until finally he made the connection. Aries's body smelled like the front yard of Alex's boyhood home after the lawn had been newly mown, green and slightly acidic, the dying shafts of grass already perfuming the air with over-rich fermentation as they began their journey of decomposition into mulch.

Abruptly, the Ram withdrew his tongue. Before Alex could draw breath, he felt both his wrists seized by one of Aries's hands while the other pushed between his back and the sheets, hauling his body upwards. With no more warning, he found himself reeling as his nostrils were overpowered by the heady cut-grass scent, so invasive that he sneezed and tried to draw back. But his captor shifted his grip and Alex, wrists now pinned behind his back, could not resist the pressure of the other hand on the rear of his head. His face was buried in the creature's armpit, and not knowing what else to do, he began to lick the flesh and hairs there.

It seemed to be what Aries wanted. He moaned and pushed Alex even deeper. Lips moist with Aries's sweat, tastes of mingled grass and clover and hay, Alex warmed to his task, avidly nibbling and licking, drawing strands of Aries's armpit hair into his mouth and sucking each drop of fragrant moisture from them before moving onto the next. In his enthusiasm, he must have bitten down slightly, for Aries grunted with annoyance and yanked his head back, throwing him back onto the bed but never loosening his grasp of Alex's wrists.

For a long moment, the Ram looked deeply into Alex's eyes, his powerful body supported on elbows and knees, stretching along the length of his captive's body but poised scant inches short of actual physical contact, looming as if to descend and crush Alex with his weight. The artist felt a light thump against his thigh; a moment later, it was repeated, this time more insistently. Aries kept searching his glance, seeming to want something from him. Alex gazed back, not knowing what was expected. He tried to surge forward, to take a nipple into his mouth, but was not permitted to move. He sought the creature's lips for another kiss but that action, too, was prevented. The thumping continued, increasing in frequency, distracting him.

Understanding was slow in coming. Aries flicked his eyes downwards, indicating Alex should look, and hoisted his body higher to give the trapped young man a clear view. The Ram's cock was now fully engorged, as massive as the rest of him and even thicker than Alex had at first thought. It was not only the hugest dick Alex had ever seen, it was the biggest he had ever imagined. A satisfied grunt brought his attention back to Aries's face, and what he saw there filled him with equal parts of delight and fear. A grin split Aries's face, revealing broad, blunt, even teeth, in an expression which Alex interpreted as selfish and more than slightly cruel.

The dick thumped against his leg again and Aries's smile broadened. With horror, Alex suddenly knew *exactly* what Aries intended to do with it.

Before he could object, before he could scream *no*, he knew the brutal strength of the creature once more. His body was lifted off the bed and, wrists still trapped, Alex was flipped in the air and slammed back down onto his stomach so hard that the wind was knocked out of him. He barely managed to yelp at the sting of his boxers being ripped away. Desperately, he clenched the muscles of his ass, knowing it was a futile defense against Aries's brutal lust. He was right.

Alex didn't realize his hands had been freed until strong arms reached around his sides and yanked him onto all fours. His back was pressed against Aries's chest and he wanted to escape, but the weight atop him forced him to support himself on his hands and knees or risk being crushed. He whimpered when he realized the shaft of the massive dick was lying along the crack of his ass, and his plaintive sounds quickly became yelps of pain when Aries's hands roved across his chest, eventually finding his nipples and pinching—hard. The pressure was like hot needles driven into his chest. He cried out; it was excruciating, yet in spite of it, he felt his body responding. Breathing hard and deep to ride the waves, he forced himself to focus on the spires of pain shooting from his poor crushed nipples down to settle at the base of his dick, prompting it to grow.

The agony in his chest was nothing compared to what came an instant later. His feeble attempts to prevent entry were ignored as the Ram thrust into him. There was no teasing, no loosening of his hole with fingers or tongue to prepare him. In a single, irresistible stroke, Aries plunged forward. Alex screamed at the fire in his asshole, his face twisted in a rictus when Aries pulled out almost the full length, then immediately reversed course, penetrating even deeper. The sensation of his ass being filled with lava spread into Alex's bowels. Tears filled his eyes and overflowed as he cried and wailed against the onslaught. His stomach and shoulder muscles clenched, his entire body shuddered until he feared he would be unable to support himself on his hands and knees for another instant. He would collapse and Aries would continue to fuck him, thrusting deeper and deeper with that humongous dick until, Alex imagined, he would be able to feel it pressing at the back of his throat from the inside.

Alex screamed again when the Ram's fingers pinched his nipples so hard they felt like they would be crushed to a pulp. But the torture to his chest worked as a kindness. At the shock of pain in front, his butt muscles involuntarily relaxed. The intense fire in his ass receded and was banked and he began to experience a more manageable and warmer sense, a flush of pleasure which consumed him, as if a broad field of summer sun-washed timothy and fern had concentrated its languid and sultry heat in his butt.

Aries continued his onslaught, abandoning his assault of Alex's chest in favor of digging his fingers into the artist's shoulders, putting his body behind each thrust and penetrating deeper. Alex's cries of pain turned to moans of pleasure. Each time the giant staff pressed against his prostate, he sensed a pulse of pressure building in his groin. His fingernails caught on the weave of the pillowcase he was clutching and ripped the fabric; he pressed his belly and cock deeper into the mattress, the sensation inside him moving toward a release which he knew would be nothing short of spectacular.

The Ram pulled out almost entirely, leaving only the huge mushroom of the tip of his dickhead still embraced by the rosebud of Alex's ass as Alex's screams of pain morphed into desperate pleas. Wiggling on his stomach, arms and legs thrashing, he begged his visitor to have mercy on him, to plunge in once again. After what seemed like an interminable delay, Aries complied. It was a swift, deep stroke, stabbing to the very center of Alex's arousal.

Alex's eyes bulged from their sockets as the Ram's penis hit home. His muscles seized for an instant, the only indication of life being a raucous gargle leaking from the back of his throat. He teetered on the edge for what seemed a long while but for what was probably only moments, knowing he was about to cum, unable to stop it, but not quite shooting yet.

The climax was explosive, a burst of hot, viscous cum pumping from the end of his dick, seeming to spring from someplace within him located much deeper than his testicles. His stomach sucked in and out with each thrust, his limbs twitching spasmodically, his ass contracted with each pulse. An inarticulate, strangled scream burst from him without warning and he bit deeply into the pillow to stifle it. The orgasm went on and on. Whenever the pulses grew weaker, Aries sensed it, pulled out and thrust again. Each time Alex thought he was completely spent, the Ram's motion squeezed more cum from his sore and aching balls until finally even the personification of the God of War must have realized he had completed his conquest.

Alex barely knew when Aries pulled out completely. He lay on his soaked bed, the sheets drenched with a combination of sweat and sperm, feeling like he'd just been ravaged by an army. Lightheaded, body sore from the abuse, he finally managed to roll onto his back, eager to embrace his newest lover and, now that the initial assault had passed, to take his time exploring that magnificent physique with his lips and hands. He longed to taste that amazing cock to find out if it mirrored the open-field flavors of the rest of the Ram's body.

But Aries was gone.

Puzzled, but not too surprised, Alex hoisted himself onto his elbows and searched the room. No one was there except the statues, all thirteen of them—including Aries—standing on their pedestals exactly where they were supposed to be. Wincing at the twinges of pain in his raw ass, and rubbing lightly around each nipple to restore the circulation, Alex sat up and swung his feet onto the floor. He stood and, hobbling into the bathroom to clean up, he grinned. If this was all only an extended fantasy, he must be a damned sight more creative than any of the art critics had given him credit for.

He showered, and afterwards, massaged some skin lotion into his chest, hoping it would reduce the tenderness. On his way back to bed, he accidentally kicked his shorts and, stooping to retrieve them, frowned. They had indeed been torn from his body but, from several experiments in rougher sex with Tony, Alex knew he'd never have had the brute strength to tear the elastic without cutting partway through with scissors first. Yet, somehow, if his therapist was right, he must have done so. Shrugging, he tossed them into a corner and lowered himself onto the damp sheets with a grimace. He knew he should change them or risk being uncomfortable until morning, but before he could drag himself to his feet again to do so, he was asleep.

Above his slumbering form, thirteen pairs of eyes looked down. The statues did not move. Their faces were partly concealed in shadow. However, in the muted light creeping in through the skylight, a few of them seemed to smile.

CHAPTER 5

"Think of it as helping out an old friend. Come on. I've never asked you for anything before."

Alex snorted and when the iced tea went down the wrong pipe, he coughed until he was red-faced and dizzy. Corey sat patiently until Alex's breathing had more or less returned to normal before wheedling again.

"If I'm staying with you, and you want to choke on something…" He cocked one eyebrow with mock lasciviousness. Evidently, he'd either spent a good deal of time in the sun during the last few days, or he'd recently started dating a stylist, because the red highlights of his hair were very hot. If Alex ignored the deep tan, the combination of raised eyebrow, newly russet hair and mischievous grin made his friend look much like an Irish leprechaun.

"I'm sorry," Alex said, "but no."

"Gimme one good reason."

Mildly amused by the not-so-thinly veiled demand, he retorted, "I don't have to. It's my place. Besides, no matter how bad the drama, you always manage to get out of it okay."

"It's not for me, buddy. It's for you." Corey forked a bit of salad into his mouth and chewed while his eyes roved past Alex's shoulder and focused on something—or more likely, *someone*—seated a few tables away. "Did you get a look at the blond guy with the hairy chest by the door?"

"Corey, stop cruising. I'm waiting to hear how your moving into *my* condo is supposed to be for my benefit."

"I'm not cruising." His tone was pettish. "I may have just fallen in love at first sight, thank you very much!" He plucked a cherry tomato from his plate and, never taking his eyes from whoever he was flirting with, he slowly licked the dressing from the fruit using only the tip of his tongue. When it was clean, he sucked it into his mouth and rolled it around obscenely before biting down, half closing his eyes as if he had just experienced the most intense orgasm of his life, and strategically allowed a trickle of juice to escape his lips so that his tongue could dart out and slurp it up before it dripped down his chin.

Alex watched his friend's antics with a smile. "That is either the grossest thing I've seen today..."

"Or an admirable display of talent." Corey interrupted cheerfully. "Sometimes, my innate skills leak out at the strangest times."

"See? You don't need to stay with me. With oral technique like that, I'm sure Mr. Hairy Blond will be begging you to move in with him by the time we're ready for coffee."

"Puh-leeze! As a trick, he's a ten. As potential husband material, I'd say less than a four. The jeans are knock-offs and the watch is a fake. I can tell even from here. But you have got to turn around and see those pecs!"

"I can see him fine in the mirror over the bar." Usually, Alex enjoyed jumping in to share Corey's fun when he was in an outlandish mood. But today, he was tired and frankly still so sore from his nocturnal imaginings of the night before that even the brief wait between ordering and being served made sitting uncomfortable.

"Seriously. I saw Nadine yesterday and she agrees with me."

"About what?" Alex allowed some exasperation to show. "What does she have to do with your wanting to move in with me for a week?"

"She's concerned. Hell, Alex, *I'm* concerned. You rent out the townhouse, buy this bizarre condo..."

"It's not bizarre."

Corey ignored him. "And spend almost every waking moment you're not at the hospital or at therapy cooped up there."

Alex thrust out his jaw. "I'm working. I need privacy."

"Maybe. But I know you better than you know yourself. I think you're brooding. Isolating. Besides..." Corey took a swig of white wine to mask his unease at what he was about to say.

"Besides...?" Alex prompted, a little piqued. He was an adult and could take care of himself. He certainly didn't need a perpetual party boy and an almost-octogenarian gallery owner watching out for him.

"I...er...stopped by your place last night."

"Duh-uh. I found you curled up in the hallway outside the front door this morning, remember? Some wild story about being locked out of your apartment because you wouldn't put out for the super? I'm sure being two months behind in your rent had nothing to do with it. I'm just surprised you didn't find some hot stud and bunk at his place."

"Waited too long for something even better to come along," Corey confessed. "Didn't find out about the lock out 'til I got home, and by then the bars were already closed and I was not about to go trawling down some alley to find some drunken toothless wonder to take me home with him."

"You could have rung the bell. I would have let you in... for the night," Alex hastened to add in case Corey decided to "creatively" interpret the statement as an invitation to show up later in the afternoon carrying everything he owned.

"You were busy." A grin and an outrageous wink followed.

"I was sleeping," Alex corrected. "It wouldn't be the first time you woke me up."

"Sleeping?" The disbelief was palpable. Corey clutched his chest like a damsel in distress, threw his head back and, to Alex's embarrassment, began carrying on dramatically. "Oh, yes. *Yes!* Oh God! *Please!* Don't stop! Ohhhaahhhooooh!" Corey arched back and rose half out of the chair, pumping his groin in mock intercourse, before collapsing back down. "Right. Sleeping."

There was a brief smattering of applause from the other diners in the restaurant at the impromptu performance, and in the mirror, Alex could see the blond man who had been the object of Corey's attention looking suitably impressed.

"The thing is..." All levity had vanished. "You were alone. At least, no one left last night. I was leaning right against the door. They would have woken me. Chilly hallways, by the way. And when you let me in this morning..."

Alex squirmed, covering his unease with another swallow of tea. "Bullshit. *If* you heard what you say you did, you would have been banging on the door itching to get inside and dive in to keep us company."

"Normally, yeah. But I figured with what you've been going through, you didn't need me spoiling your fun." He batted his eyelashes coquettishly. "You have to admit I'm much prettier than you are and I didn't want you to be left out once your trick got a look at my beautiful bod."

"There…was…no…trick," Alex said through gritted teeth.

Corey nodded. "I realized that this morning. So, that leaves only one thing." He lowered his voice to a very loud stage whisper and pitched it in the direction of the blond he'd been cruising. "Masturbation!"

"Keep your voice *down!*"

"Why? D'you think anyone *here* would be offended?" He made a great show of inspecting the other restaurant patrons—almost all of whom were youngish gay men wearing as little as legally possible in the way of clothing so as to show off their bodies to better advantage. The remaining diners were mostly well-outfitted gray-haired gay men, sipping white wine and goggling at the aforementioned younger boys sitting at neighboring tables.

Corey made sure to blow a kiss to the hairy blond when their eyes met and smirked when the young man flushed fire-engine red.

"I don't think I like you spying at my front door," Alex said, not amused.

"I don't think I like you feeling you've gotta jerk off—and from the sound, it was quite a jerk—just because you're having issues about Tony."

"What's wrong with jerking off?"

Corey held up a finger. "One. Nothing. Two." Another finger joined the first. "You've got someone right in front of you who would gladly take care of things for you. No strings attached. Three. What I heard last night…well, I would have bet my truck there was someone with you. It sounded so…real. I *know* you don't watch porn so…Fantasizing is healthy, Alex, but what

I heard was way too intense to be…I dunno…" He shrugged before suggesting. "…healthy?"

Alex frowned but, before he could snap at his friend, Corey barreled on. "If I'm there, I can keep an eye on you. Cheer you up. You might even find yourself having—God forbid!—a little fun? You know, the way we used to. Even without the sex we always had a great time together. Besides…" He looked at Alex with a grin. "I really *do* need someplace to stay. At least for tonight. Tomorrow, I can make nicey-nicey with the super and whore my way back into my place long enough to get my stuff."

"And tomorrow night?"

"Wannamaker's gonna be at Nadine's again tomorrow, right? Charles has always got a spare room I can sack out in for a few days. All I gotta do is let him blow me and…" He grinned. "He may be older than I like, but with age comes experience— so they say—and the guy's got a truly talented mouth. I think," he said, with cartoonish bravery, "I can handle the sacrifice."

"One night? You're sure?"

"It will be a night to remember, I promise you." Corey's grin was practically a leer.

"I am *not* having sex with you, Corey."

Inadvertently, Alex had spoken too loudly. At Corey's pretended crestfallen look, an old queen at an adjoining tabled called out, "If he won't, honey, I will!" and the hairy-chested blond looked distinctly hopeful.

"I warn you," Alex said. "One hand on my thigh and I'm dumping you onto the floor."

"Don't worry. From the looks of things…" He inclined his head to indicate the blond. "…I might fall in love this afternoon. What do you say to a three-way?" Corey seemed like a little kid begging mommy for a toy. Alex knew the cuteness was studied, but nevertheless he found he couldn't fully resist it. "Corey, I'm warning you." Alex was unable to repress a smile.

"Gotta keep in practice for Wannamaker!" Corey chirped merrily.

"What am I getting myself into?" Alex wondered aloud.

"Like I said," Corey winked. "A night to remember."

For both of them, his words would prove all too true.

In less than an hour, it was as if Alex and Corey had never ceased being college roommates. The two had known each other so long and so well, and were so used to each other's quirks, that the transition was seamless. They'd managed to sneak back into Corey's apartment and retrieve most of his clothing. In his quest for perpetual trendiness, Corey rarely held on to any garment for more than one season except for the odd T-shirt, so his entire wardrobe barely filled half the trunk of Alex's Saab. The furniture would have to wait until Corey had made amends to the superintendent. If reconciliation wasn't possible, Alex was pretty sure Corey would just abandon it without a backwards glance.

Within seconds of arriving at the condo, Corey dumped a tangle of jeans and shirts into a corner. Alex pointedly went to the closet and took out a few hangers, which Corey ignored in favor of stripping to the waist, pouring himself a glass of wine and flopping on the sofa in front of the television. Sighing, Alex made a perfunctory effort to slip a few shirts onto hangers before abandoning the idea in favor of bundling them up and stowing them at the bottom of one of the closets. Thus were their old habits re-established.

"I'm gonna run over to the townhouse and see if there's any mail," Alex said. "I'll stop at the store and pick us up something for dinner, so do me a favor and don't order pizza."

Corey waved, absorbed in a rerun of *The Golden Girls*. Wondering yet again what he was thinking when he agreed to let his friend stay, Alex locked the condo door behind himself.

The tenants at the townhouse, a gay couple who were longtime clients of Tony's, were both home when Alex arrived. Though Alex was reluctant to disturb them and wanted to return home and interrupt any potential chaos Corey had gotten into while he was gone, the couple was anxious for news of Tony's condition. Adding to the delay was the younger of the two's eagerness for Alex to sample some new hors d'oeuvres he'd recently created for his catering company's revised menu. Between the canapés forced on him and the lengthy gossip over several cups of tea, the five minutes Alex had planned to spend with them turned into almost two hours. Once he'd extricated himself, he met with further delays due to long lines at the supermarket. He'd also noticed that Corey's container of protein powder, religiously imbibed twice daily, seemed almost empty. Feeling generous toward his friend, Alex dropped into the health food store to pick up another with some idea of removing the burden from Corey of having to fork out thirty or forty dollars from his own pocket in order to replenish the supply. But the computers controlling the cash register were temporarily down and the original thirty minutes he'd planned to be gone turned into close to four hours.

By the time he got back to the condo in the old library, Alex was tired, hot, irritated and wanted nothing more than to strip out of the clothes stuck to his body with drying sweat and step into a cool shower. Arms laden with grocery bags, he elbowed the door open and opened his mouth to yell for Corey to help him. When he saw what was going on in the center of the room, the words dried up in his throat.

Alex knew immediately who it was. His eyes flicked to the pedestal above his head and he frowned, puzzled. Though the identity of the naked man Corey was kneeling in front of was unmistakable, his stone twin was still gazing down from above. The grocery bags slid forgotten to the floor; the door swung shut behind him unnoticed. Alex stood in the entryway dumbly, unable to do anything but drink in the beauty of Corey's strange visitor.

Though he was slim, his nudity revealed a taut, muscular body—the chest, arms and shoulders lean and powerful. A cappuccino tan covered him from head to toe, coating even those areas not normally exposed to the sun, as was revealed when Corey shifted position and Alex could feast his eyes on more of the vision's amazing flesh. From beneath the skin, a healthy ruddy glow emanated, as if the young man had spent years running naked across a primeval savannah under a blazing sun. And though Alex normally found himself attracted to smooth-skinned men, at the exhibition of a mat of lush hair the color of dark honey covering the man's chest and stomach, he felt his own dick stiffen and begin to press against his slacks. When

Corey paused, glancing over his shoulder at Alex with a pleased grin, he could see the hairiness wasn't limited to the torso. The thighs and legs were lush with a tawny down contrasting with the thatch of darker sienna pierced by an elegantly slim dick of astonishing length.

"Welcome to the party, stranger," Corey quipped. "We were just passing the time while we waited for you."

In a daze, Alex stepped forward, one hand reaching without conscious volition. He ached to run his fingers across the man's chest, to feel the silkiness of it, to bury his face there and inhale what he already knew would be a feral scent redolent with dry heat and muted musk. The newcomer smiled, revealing painfully white teeth with incisors just a little too long and sharp to be quite human. His eyes were the virgin green of newly unfurled palm leaves, and as Alex drew closer, he saw slit pupils surrounded by an aura of glowing amber.

Perhaps Corey had been distracted from the oddly feline eyes by the man's hair. Billowing down past his shoulders, it was a veritable mane, the strands plump and glistening with vibrant health, in shades of earthy brunette from copper-blond through fawn, past umber tinged with rust and blending into a dark, well-oiled mahogany. Alex had a brief mental flash of the man reclining on the bed, his hair spread out in a halo around him in an erotic contrast between the lush browns and the stark whiteness of the sheets. But he knew this man—this otherworldly creature—could never be so passive as to merely lie back.

No, in the young man's carriage, in the sharp intelligence of his handsome face, in the way he gazed at Alex with regal confidence, it was clear that though he demanded and was accustomed to worship, Leo would receive the loving attention of his supplicants whilst standing firmly on his feet so he could look down on those who lavished their adoration upon him with kingly approval.

With a sparse movement of his hand indicating the floor in front of him, a motion of command used to being obeyed, Leo acknowledged his readiness to accept Alex as one of his own. The sublime arrogance of the man was palpable and something Alex normally would have bristled at, but a sense of indulgent kindness accompanied it. *Do what I wish*, Leo seemed to say silently, *and I will shield you and protect you from all harm.*

Alex found himself on his knees, not knowing how he'd gotten there, humbled and servile in the face of Leo's majesty, gazing up at him with adoration. Though standing Alex would have been topped him by at least six inches, looking up at Leo, he fancied the Lion was taller and that the top of his head was surrounded by a golden corona of light. He barely registered Corey's hands plucking at the buttons of his shirt, so transfixed was he by the vision in front of him, and realized he had been stripped to the waist only when he felt the cooler air in the room soothing his sweaty back and chest, seeming to wash away the grit of the city and to ease the fatigue in his shoulders and back from lugging the heavy bags of groceries upstairs.

He shuffled forward, halting at Corey's murmured, "Wait," and knelt while his friend unhooked his belt, unzipped his fly and rolled his trousers down to gather at his bent knees. His shoes and socks were already gone; he hadn't noticed them being taken off. Corey moved behind him and tugged at the cuffs sharply. Alex had to put out his hands palm-down on the marble floor to keep from pitching facedown upon it. His trousers were removed swiftly and Alex felt suddenly vulnerable, kneeling before the raw and primal power of this beautiful, hairy man. Some overwhelming impulse, some inner psychic voice told him not to rise, but to remain where he was. Overcome by a desire to please him, Alex knew how to make Leo happy. Without hesitation, he lowered himself to the floor and remained there, completely naked and stretched full length in prostration at the feet of his kingly visitor.

Leo sighed, contented, his delight at Alex's worship obvious. Inching forward, only scant inches intervened before Alex's forehead made contact with the Lion's feet, slim and shapely, the tops graced with scattered strands of that marvelous silken hair, the nails darker than normal but perfectly formed. Hesitant, Alex's tongue crept out. He licked one toe tentatively and was rewarded with a grunt of approval from Leo and the heady taste of good rich earth, recently turned, now slowly baking and drying beneath an equatorial sun.

His tongue washed between the toes of one foot, then the other, creeping upwards to dally at the soft down covering the Lion's calves and thighs. Up his mouth moved, ever up, until he found his face buried in the tufts of hair covering Leo's balls—a mane that matched the one on his head. Alex took one ping-pong-ball-sized testicle into his mouth, rolling his tongue around it as if it were a giant grape to be savored, encasing it in the moist warmth of his saliva. Opening his jaw wider, he amazed himself that he was able to encompass both balls. At the same time, his hands sought the creature's firm-muscled ass to steady himself so he could take the testicles even deeper into his mouth. Alex allowed his fingertips to trace the rosebud of Leo's hole and was rewarded with a delicious shudder as Leo spread his legs slightly wider and put both hands on Alex's shoulders to steady himself.

Now Alex's fingers were slick with the sweat trickling down the lion-man's back and moistening the round, perfect globes of his butt. Mischievously, Alex applied pressure with one index finger, seeking to probe the hole, but he winced when Leo dug his fingernails into Alex's shoulders to express his disapproval. Clearly, the king was not to be fucked—even with a finger—and Alex resigned himself to the limitations, delightful though they might be, of a purely oral exploration.

His mouth opened to allow the huge balls to dangle free for an instant before grasping them in his hands and kneading gently. At the same time, he drew his tongue from the underside of the base of the penis's shaft, slowly up the length to the tip. When he reached the hole at the end, he nipped lightly—not to cause pain but to tantalize—while at the same time massaging Leo's testicles harder while tugging them a bit. The moan he elicited sounded suspiciously like a soft growl.

Leo's dick oozed not a drop of pre-cum, but Alex's own made up for the lack. He could feel the moist, hot juices seeping from the end. When he moved and his dick brushed against his thigh, his leg was sticky with it. He could feel the pressure building in his testicles like a river backing up behind a dam, roiling and churning, aching for the floodgates to be opened. He thought about using one hand to grab his own dick, to stroke it roughly, to pull himself until a stream of cum shot from the end. But when he made a movement to do so, Leo's fingers tightened once again, this time hard enough to make Alex wince. Obviously, a majestic pleasure would be gratified before the needs of mere mortals.

Alex increased his attentions, taking the entire dick into his mouth and bobbing his head back and forth—down slow to the root of Leo's cock, where the pubic hairs tickled Alex's nose, then swiftly back along the column's length until only his lips met around the very tip. Over and over he repeated the motion, adding all the variations he had ever learned from other lovers. The Lion's grunts of pleasure became more pronounced, and his hips thrust forward to meet each of Alex's onslaughts on his dick. Alex would have sworn he could literally feel the jism building in the Lion's balls, preparing to explode forth down Alex's throat or spatter his face with its searing heat while filling his nostrils with its earthy, mushroom-like smell.

Leo pumped and the growls deep in his chest grew until he was practically roaring in pleasure. But aside from a liberal coating of Alex's saliva, his dick remained dry. Though Alex's enthusiasm was not flagged in the least, his jaw was sore and his neck muscles were starting to stiffen. He sought to pull back, to rest for a brief moment, but Leo's hands, now clutching at the back of Alex's head, urged him on, forced him not to stop.

All the while, the urge to shoot was becoming more maddening with every second. Desperately, Alex clenched the muscles of his butt and groin. Perhaps if the contractions could shake his own dick, causing it to slap against his thigh fast enough, he could achieve release. But unless he could supply his cock with some kind of actual friction, Alex knew he was doomed to suffer.

Just when the pressure in his balls was becoming unbearable, Alex sensed a familiar presence slip between Leo's legs from the rear. Glancing down as best he could given his position, he saw Corey lying on his back, wearing the widest grin Alex had ever seen. Before he could figure out what was going on, Corey reached up and grabbed Alex's cheeks, at the same time burying his face in the sensitive area between his asshole and the base of his cock. An instant later, Alex shuddered as Corey's tongue began to lap at the very bottom of his balls. The sensation was so torturous, and Corey's actions so deliciously sadistic, Alex gasped, momentarily forgetting the dick in his mouth.

At that precise instant, Leo's body surged forward, toppling Alex over backwards, his dick plunging so far down Alex's throat that he feared he would suffocate. Simultaneously, Corey twisted around and, without preamble, swallowed Alex's dick to the root, grabbing his balls and squeezing them as if they were a tube of toothpaste and he needed to eject the last bit of paste.

The lion atop him, his best friend below him, the sensation grew past the point where it was possible for him to stand it any longer. A hot, lurid bubble formed in his gut and swelled, sending shafts of shivering electricity past the clenched muscles of his stomach, across his heaving chest, up the back of his throat as if he had swallowed a current that was seeking to find the dick in his mouth. At the same time, the heat spread from his balls to the end of his dick in a white-hot stream of pleasure.

Moaning and begging as best he could through a mouthful of cock, pleading for the two of them to take pity on him, Alex exploded. Streaky ribbons of scalding sperm shot from the end of his dick, arcing several feet in the air. He imagined he could literally hear the hiss of cooling jism when it splattered against the cold marble of the floor. Simultaneously, with a mighty roar, Leo shot his own load, pumping what seemed like quarts of thick cum down Alex's throat. Faster and faster, the beast rocked his hips. Alex swallowed desperately, trying to keep up. But the King of the Jungle's orgasm showed no sign of stopping. Worse, even though Corey knew Alex was the type to only cum once without a rest between orgasms, the russet-haired young man started in on Alex's dick in earnest.

Alex cried. He screamed. He begged. Every nerve in his body felt as if it were firing in rapid overload. His fingers clutched at Leo's hips, seeking to move him away, but the Lion's skin was sweat-slicked and too slippery to get a decent hold and Alex resorted to pushing frantically at his stomach. But Leo's stomach muscles were like the armor plates of a tank and

Alex's attempts were futile. He squirmed, trying to slide away from Corey's mouth, but his friend was merciless, licking and nibbling at his dick, massaging his balls to drive out the last, minuscule dregs of cum. Alex's heels drummed at the floor in protest. His shoulders slapped against the marble, each contact propelling drops of his sweat in all directions.

Then miraculously, time seemed to slow. The sensations grew no less—they increased, in fact—but Alex suddenly found himself in sync. His frantic gyrations to get away eased, the motions smoothing out, synchronizing with the thrusts of the cock down his throat and the slide of Corey's mouth up and down his dick. In amazement, he felt the gathering in his groin again. This time, it was no mere sluice gate opening. This time, it was like flood waters after they had burst their banks, flowing in a huge deluge down the riverbed, slowly and inexorably with a deceptive smoothness and false tranquility until they smashed against an obstruction in their way.

And smash they did, obliterating the last vestiges of Alex's control. In the instant before he shot his second load—when it had not yet happened but would have needed a miracle to stop— Alex found his mouth empty, the massive cock withdrawn to be replaced with the moist, tender Saharan heat of the Lion's lips. The taste of his strangely rough-surfaced tongue, musky and feline, smelling of overheated air and arid breezes, was enough to drive Alex past the brink.

His orgasm was tremendous; it was like he had not already cum once. This time he shot not in ribbons, but in great gouts. Dollops of hot, steaming sperm propelled themselves through the air like missiles. God, it hurt! His balls ached like they'd been trapped in a vise, and his stomach muscles tightened to painful levels. The torrent of sperm rushing through his dick felt wide enough to rupture it, to shred it like a blunderbuss exploding in the hands of some Saturday-morning cartoon character. On and on it went for what seemed like hours until finally, sore and physically drained, he closed his eyes, and for several moments he lost consciousness.

When he came to, he could hear Corey ushering their guest out the door. There was the brief rustle of cloth against naked flesh and the door closed with a soft thump. A moment later, Corey squatted next to Alex's shoulder. Without turning his head, the exhausted artist could see Corey's shaven balls dangling between his legs. His friend's dick was softening, but still plump and partially tumescent.

"Do I bring you great presents, or what?" Corey grinned.

"Where...?" Alex had to pause to swallow and clear his parched throat. "Where did you find him?"

"Where?" Corey seemed puzzled by the question. "Um... at the bar? Or, maybe...No. Walking down the street?" He frowned, struggling to remember, and then dismissed the question with an airy wave of his hand. "What does it matter?" He leaned forward and planted an affectionate kiss on Alex's still moist brow. "If there are any more out there as hot as that one, I'd drag 'em in from out of garbage cans if I had to!"

"Did you get his name?" Alex croaked. There was no doubt of the man's identity and Alex was concerned. This was the first time—aside from his Virgo fantasy at the hospital—that one of the Zodiac Men had come into his life from outside the apartment. The interludes seemed to be getting more and more real. He feared he could no longer relegate them to the realms of his subconscious. If not for Corey's participation, he would be worried about his sanity.

"Name?" his friend scoffed. "Who needs names with a body like that? Come on." He reached out to clasp Alex's forearm to haul him to his feet. "You could use a wash, and..." His eyes glinted mischievously. "Some company in the shower."

Alex groaned painfully as he allowed Corey to help him to his feet, wondering where his old roommate could possibly summon the strength to even suggest playing in the shower. After his antics of a few minutes ago, Alex doubted he could even stand under the water without having to lean against the side of the stall to hold himself up.

Corey observed his exhaustion and took mild pity on him. "No worries. I'll just scrub your back. You don't look like you could do anything anyway. We'll save the lather and rinse of more interesting parts of your body for after you recover."

Leaning heavily on Corey's shoulder as they made their way

to the bathroom, Alex reflected that, again, during the entirety of their intimacy, he had not heard Leo speak a word. Standing under the spray with Corey lavishly soaping him from head to toe, he found himself wondering why.

CHAPTER 6

The silver-haired nurse was on duty again, plumping pillows in an ineffective effort to make her charge more comfortable, when Alex arrived at the ICU.

"Any change?" he asked half-heartedly and not expecting an answer different from the one he'd gotten on his last few visits.

The nurse just smiled, encouraging and sympathetic, and busied herself refilling the water pitcher and straightening the tray table. "I got you some sodas," she told him kindly once she'd finished her duties and was paused in the doorway ready to leave. "Orange, right? I remember you brought some with you a few times. I guessed that's your favorite."

"Can't stand the taste," Alex replied without thinking. "Too sweet. They were…they *are* Tony's favorite though, so…"

She placed one reassuring hand on his shoulder. "I understand, sweetie. You two just sit here and have a nice long chat. The doctor will be making rounds in a little while. We can always hope he'll have good news for you."

After she'd left, he sat for a while silently, his thoughts whirling around inside his head, colliding with each other and only confusing him more. When Tony's motionlessness had grown too intense, when the almost imperceptible hiss of the respirator became so annoying it made him want to smash it, when the muted sounds of nurses and relatives passing in the hallway seemed to grow to a dull roar, Alex blurted out, "I think I'm going crazy."

Tony did not, of course, respond. Alex sat for a few minutes patiently, as if waiting for Tony to consider his statement, gather his thoughts and answer him with just the right words to show him how silly the statement really was. As the minutes dragged on, Alex began to fidget, feeling guilty and not knowing why, until finally he was compelled to speak again.

"The first one, Virgo, was just a daydream. I know that. I just wanted…I wanted…" A sob caught in his throat. "I wanted us to be together again so badly. When the merman came to me, I thought it was just a hallucination from the paint fumes. But then, after Aries, I found a pair of my briefs on the floor. I remember having them torn off me and I *know* I couldn't have done it myself. But…" He shrugged. "Maybe it was adrenaline. Like those women who lift cars off their babies. Maybe I'm even more upset about…" He waved his hand to indicate the length of Tony's still form. "…about *this* than I realized. So, I thought, adrenaline's the answer. But yesterday, Corey brought this guy home. For a three-way."

The guilt overwhelmed him again.

"I'd never have done it, honey, if you were *here*. If you were with me. I told him I didn't want to, but you know how Corey is. He's got this idea that sex will help me take my mind off what's going on. That sex will take care of almost anything and…" His voice trailed off for a moment before he resumed, his tone expressing his awe at the memory. "It was Leo. Oh, Tony, he was beautiful. I know it sounds cliché but he was like some savage beast, beautiful and dangerous at the same time. There was something else about him. I don't know how to describe it…I guess you could say he was sort of…noble. The weird thing was, this time I checked the statues and the Leo was still up on his pedestal while the guy was standing in the apartment." He laughed bitterly. "I was crazy enough to start thinking they were somehow coming to life. But with Leo right there and Corey, well, helping things out, I figured at least *this* one was real. Maybe I was hallucinating, or fantasizing or whatever, but if there was an actual guy in the room, I couldn't be that far around the bend. Confused maybe, but not completely insane. But then I mentioned him to Corey this morning and do you know what?"

He paused again, waiting for the answer that never came.

"Corey had *no* idea what I was talking about! According to

him, I went out for a few hours, came back with some groceries and we had dinner—that's all. He doesn't remember Leo—he swears we didn't have sex—he said he wanted to but I looked too tired. He doesn't even remember that we took a shower together afterwards like we used to do in college. He says he spent the whole afternoon watching TV on the couch while I cooked. He was even able to tell me which episodes he saw, not like that means anything because he's seen them all a hundred times and can quote 'em from start to finish. Oh, Tony..." he wailed. "What's *wrong* with me?"

"Stress, if you ask me."

Alex whirled. He hadn't realized he'd risen and was clutching one of Tony's hands. A man in his mid-thirties wearing a white coat stood in the hospital room doorway. Alex blushed and sputtered for a minute. Though he might doubt his own sanity, he wasn't sure what the doctor had overheard and had no desire to be locked up in a straitjacket in a rubber room.

"Heya, Joey," he stammered.

"That's *Doctor* Joey to you, boy," he said with mock severity. "Show some respect for eight years of med school, will ya?"

He came into the room and checked the charts and fiddled with some dials while he spoke. "You sound like you've been through the mill, kiddo. Not that I blame you. Tony's in no discomfort—I'm making sure of that. But you...when the heck are you gonna come clean and admit how rough this is on *you*?"

"How much did you hear?"

Joey frowned and punched the touchpad of one of the machines until the dial reading met with his satisfaction. "Just something about Corey's shenanigans. And you feeling like you were going crazy—which is perfectly natural with what you're dealing with. If you ask me, Corey's the one who should be tied to a psychiatrist's couch, not you. If we're lucky, we could find him a shrink who'd prescribe a chastity belt for him. And a muzzle."

Joe Caprese was an old flame of Tony's from way back before he and Alex had met. The two had dated for a while and got along splendidly. They still did. But in spite of their commitment to make things work between them, they found they were sexually incompatible. While both Tony and Alex considered themselves "versatile" and switched positions with enthusiastic erotic abandon, Joey was an exclusive "bottom" and after a while, Tony had later confessed to Alex, their sex life had gotten monotonous.

"He's a doctor, for Pete's sake!" Tony had complained. "You'd think he'd know his way around the human body, right?"

Having no issues outside the bedroom, and legitimately enjoying each other's company, Tony and Joey had stayed friends. Once Alex came into the picture, they would frequently go out together as a group—Tony, Alex, Joey and whatever sweet young thing Joey was dating at the moment. Joey was the type who was incessantly searching for a husband, and seemed never able to find a relationship to last more than a few weeks. Very probably, the fact that as he grew older he found himself attracted to younger and younger men was part of the problem. The last one he'd brought to dinner, scarcely two weeks before Tony had been taken ill, looked like he was barely twenty-one.

At one point, Alex and Tony conceived the misbegotten idea that they should introduce their respective best friends to each other. Joey would provide financial and emotional stability to the relationship, which Corey desperately needed. In turn, Corey might loosen the doctor up a little; Joey often complained that he *knew* he was retentive but couldn't seem to do anything about it. Besides, even though Corey was a decade or so older than most of Joey's dates, he was exactly the doctor's physical type. In theory, it was a match made in heaven.

In reality, it had been like trying to mix oil and vinegar. The two men were obviously physically attracted to each other; that was obvious from the instant they met. But within a remarkably short time, Corey's frivolousness started wearing on Joey's nerves and he started making subtly sarcastic comments about overgrown children. For his part, Corey found Joey's innate reserve to be stuck up and pretentious, and predictably couldn't help poking fun at him and jacking up his antics to new heights just to see what kind of reaction he could provoke.

The evening had not gone well and, later that night, Alex and Tony had made a pact and resolved never to try anything like it again. Nevertheless, though Corey and Joey would never be close, they'd managed to work out a tolerable truce between them—mostly so that the four of them could get together in public as friends without driving Alex and Tony crazy with their incessant posturing and bickering.

"Hmmm, I don't like these uremic levels."

A blast of panic overtook Alex. "What?"

"Oh, sorry." Joey grimaced at his indiscretion. "Thinking aloud. Nothing to worry about yet. Still…" He glanced down at the chart and shook his head. "I'm thinking putting him on dialysis might be a good idea."

"Dialysis?" Alex felt a wave of terror wash over him.

Joey hastened to calm him. "It's just a precaution, Alex," he soothed. "His urine output has dropped over the past few days. His kidneys *seem* fine but I don't want to take chances. Dialysis will take the stress off them. We talked about this possibility, remember?"

"When we were going over the health care authorization thingies?"

"Medical power of attorney. Yeah. Besides…" He patted Tony's shoulder affectionately. "I've always been jealous that you got to marry the most beautiful man I ever met. We don't want that pretty face getting all bloated and puffy. Tony would kill me if I let that happen."

"When do you want to do this?"

Joey hesitated a fraction of a second before venturing, "Now would probably be a good time."

Alex felt his heart sink.

"Don't look so glum, Alex. Taking the burden from his kidneys might help his body to marshal the resources to beat this thing."

"This thing? The thing no one seems to know what it is."

"Doctors aren't perfect, Alex," Joey said, sighing. "We do the best we can with what we know. Hell, you'd think after three thousand years of medical science we'd know our way around the human body by now, wouldn't you?"

Alex's eyes widened at Joey's unconscious echo of the joke Tony had made so often but decided it had just been coincidence.

"I'll get the forms for you to sign and we'll get him hooked up right away. I want you to look at me, Alex."

Reluctantly, Alex met Joey's eyes.

"I'm not going to let anything happen to him if I can help it. I promise you. Do you understand me?"

Alex nodded, miserable.

"I'll be right back. Stay here. You can wait in the lounge until we're finished with Tony and then..." He glanced at his watch. "I'm off shift in about twenty minutes. I'm taking you out for a bite and you can tell Doctor Joey all about this silly notion you have that you're going crazy. Don't budge 'til I get back. Doctor's orders."

An hour and a half later, Alex was listlessly toying with the remains of a slice of peach cobbler, picking bits of crust up with his fork, setting them back down untasted and shifting the gooey peaches around the plate.

"If you were in the mood for mush, Alex, you could have ordered it," Joey said. "I'm sure the chef would have come up with something."

"Just not hungry, I guess."

"I'm not surprised."

Throughout the meal, Joey had been urging him to eat while Alex just picked at his plate. Undaunted, Joey kept ordering different dishes, hoping one of them would pique his friend's appetite. Now they sat with enough food on the table to feed five people, but aside from a few leaves of salad and a taste of the cobbler, none of it had made its way into Alex's mouth.

Exasperated, the doctor tried one final time. "You're too thin, boy-o. If you don't eat at least one bite of that dessert, I'm gonna have you involuntarily committed to my care and force-feed you."

"Fine," Alex snapped and defiantly shoveled a large forkful into his mouth, pretending to chew with overacted gusto and managing somehow to make himself swallow. "Satisfied?" He pushed his plate away and folded his arms across his chest stubbornly.

"Don't you stick that chin out at me, young man."

"Don't *you* keep shaking that fork in my face."

The doctor gave up with a huge sigh of defeat. "At least I got a few glasses of red wine into you. They say it's supposed to be healthy, but all I know is it tastes good." He pushed back his own plate and dabbed at his mouth with a napkin. "Now, about these visions you say you're having..."

With artful skill, Joey had spent most of lunch working his way past Alex's initial resistance to talk about what he'd experienced. By the time the main course had arrived—and Alex was well into his second glass of wine—Alex had started to confess. Once he began, the words rushed out of him, and by dessert, Alex had told Joey practically everything. He'd been careful, however, to edit his account so all the elements of realism, all the physical evidence that the hallucinations had *not* been merely fantasy, were absent from the telling.

"It's all perfectly natural, it seems to me," the doctor said.

"Everyone keeps telling me that."

"By everyone, you mean Cheryl?" Joey snorted with derision. "Ever since she changed her last name to Dawn-Squirrel, my opinion of her has dropped into the toilet. Not that it was ever high to begin with."

"It's her spirit animal. She first came to her at dawn. It makes perfect sense to me."

"It's a *girl* squirrel?" Joey rolled his eyes. "How'd she find that out? Pick it up and look underneath?"

Cheryl was a longstanding subject of argument between them. The doctor had his feet planted in logic and reality as firmly as two oak tree trunks while the therapist's head, in Joey's opinion, was drifting in some disembodied stupor up in the firmament.

"She's holistic, Joey. Mind affects body and vice versa. They've been doing this sort of thing in China for thousands of years. Just because Western medicine doesn't..." From the politely blank look on his face, Alex could see the shutters of Joey's mind were already firmly closed. "Look, I don't want to have this conversation with you again. Not right now."

Joey ignored him and persisted. "Good. You know I don't hold with this New Age touchy-feely stuff she's into. Give me a good Jungian analyst any day. Have you ever been to her house? Crystals and tarot cards all over the place. And…" His nose wrinkled with distaste. "What's with those cats? How many does she have? Ten? Twenty?"

"Three."

"Seems like more. Sure as hell stinks like it. If you ask me, Cheryl's a crazy Cat Lady in the making."

"Lay off, will ya? She helps me, doesn't she?"

"Not if you're hallucinating, she doesn't. What's her prescribed course of treatment? Lighting candles and meditating on your karma? Rain dances? I'm surprised Missy Dawn-Squirrel doesn't have you traipsing around her office in a deerskin loincloth waving a tomahawk."

"Something like that." Alex grinned weakly at the image.

The therapist's spiritual oddities had infiltrated every aspect of her life—except the way she dressed. No matter how much she might secretly want to dangle crystals and pagan religious symbols from long chains around her neck and weave feathers through her hair, she was well aware that the success of her practice depended on presenting a professional demeanor to the world at large, a professionalism made even more vital by the unconventionality of her techniques. Alex had often kidded her that her penchant for rigidly tailored designer suits—all in natural fabrics, of course—virtually guaranteed she'd never attract the kind of New Age, Peace Corps-volunteering girls she preferred to bed. The wealthy Long Island lesbian look, Alex tried to convince her, would frighten them off. He couldn't deny she was more than kooky, to be sure, but underneath, he was convinced she was a damned good therapist.

"Lemme put my two cents in," Joey said. "It's not uncommon for people to go all Linda Lovelace when they're trying to deal with their grief. It's like opening up an emotional pressure valve to let the excess steam out. Sometimes when you're confronted with death, you try to reaffirm life. What better way to do that than with sex?"

"Death?" Alex cried out with alarm. "But, you said…Tony's not…!"

"No, no, no. That's not what I meant," Joey hastened to correct himself. "I'm not talking about anyone actually dying.

I mean, when we're faced with the *possibility* of death and..." He spoke faster to say what he wanted to say before Alex could misinterpret him again. "...Any time someone we love is sick with a serious illness, even if it's something they'll recover from—as I'm optimistic Tony will eventually—the emotions we experience are the same as if we'd already lost them."

Alex breathed a sigh of relief. For a moment, he'd thought...

"It's human nature for some people to want to fuck when we're confronted with that kind of loss," Joey continued. "Look, kiddo, you're a highly sexual guy. Not as sexual as *some* people—and you *know* who I mean. At least you're responsible about what you do with your dick. Guys like Corey, on the other hand, must have Teflon assholes. Otherwise, it'd be him who you were visiting in a hospital bed."

"He takes precautions." Alex often felt he had to defend his friend against Joey's prudishness.

"And you should too. If, that is, you ever decide to actually go out and do something aside from dream about it—no matter how real the dreams seem to you. Look, you moved into this place with dozens of these obscene statues staring down at you and..."

"They're not obscene. They're beautiful. They're art. If anyone should be able to recognize art when they see it, it's me. Besides, there's only *one* dozen, not dozens."

"Whatever." Joey dismissed Alex's protests with a casual wave. "Don't you see the connection, how they triggered your subconscious?"

"I suppose," Alex slowly ventured, not buying the explanation for an instant, yet wanting to believe it very badly.

"I'm no tofu-eating, crystal-gazing, herbal lesbian therapist like Cheryl, but it seems to me she's gotten the gist of things right. Even if I'm not wild about the ways she explains things," he grumbled. "Get your ass back into the gym, at least, will you? Start cruising some flesh-and-blood gods instead of salivating over a few hunks of marble. You've lost weight and you're pale. The exercise will do you good. Tag along with Corey. At least he's good for *that.*"

Joey took a sip from his coffee and grimaced before

motioning to a waiter. "Cold already. So…" He changed the subject. "How's the work going? You spending enough time at the easel? No creative blocks?"

"Actually, I think the stress is making me more creative than normal."

"That makes sense." He nodded sagely. "Painting helps you release the tension so you can function. A lot of artists are like that, or so I'm told. I wouldn't know. I can barely draw a straight line. The interns are always complaining my handwriting sucks."

"Just like your bedside manner?" Alex asked archly.

"Now, *that's* the old sarcastic asshole we all know and love." Joey grinned. "You know, since your work is so cathartic for you, it occurs to me…"

"What?"

The thought was interrupted by the arrival of a fresh cup of coffee. Joey busied himself adding non-dairy creamer and ersatz sugar, tasting repeatedly until it met his satisfaction.

"That's so annoying."

Joey looked at him, questioning.

"The way you put in like a quarter packet of that sugar shit, sip it, make a face, add cream, sip it again, make a *worse* face, dump in more, and keep doing it over and over again until it's sludge. It's not like you don't always put in three packs of sugar and half a thingy of cream every time."

"What's the point of drinking it if it's not the way I like it?"

Alex stuck his tongue out at the light beige beverage in Joey's cup. "What's the point of drinking it at all the way you gussy it up?"

"You're trying to distract me, Alex."

The artist fluttered his eyelashes, feigning innocence.

"We were taking about catharsis and I think…" Joey paused, clearly uncertain of how to make the suggestion without provoking a reaction, while Alex waited expectantly.

"I think, maybe…you should try painting one of *them*."

Alex took an uncharacteristically long time setting up. No matter how he shifted the easel supporting the blank canvas, he couldn't seem to get it illuminated properly. He angled it several different ways, but each time he thought he was ready to begin, the skylight frame would cause his shadow to fall across it and obscure the area where he'd intended to start work. When finally, it was satisfactorily placed, Alex found some of his brushes had stiffened. Annoyed with himself for neglecting to clean them properly, he shoved them aside and took out his pencils. Though he rarely sketched the image onto the canvas before starting in with the oils, he thought that this time, given his conflicted emotions about his subject, easing into things might be best.

Corey had popped his head into the condo only briefly. It seemed the rift between him and his apartment superintendent was irreparable—mostly due to Corey's inability to pay the rent but, in no small part also because Corey had steadfastly refused to allow the super to fuck him. Fortunately, the gorgeous reprobate had run into Charles Wannamaker when he'd stopped by the Shermer Gallery to bother Nadine with the sad and sordid story of his woes and to pester her for a cash loan. Charles had leaped at the opportunity to have a houseguest. Corey had grabbed only a couple of T-shirts and his gym bag, and borrowed a decent pair of Alex's slacks—in case Charles insisted on taking him to a nice restaurant, he'd explained to Alex with a wink—and rushed out with the vague commitment to pick up the rest of his things "soon."

While he fussed about arranging and rearranging his paints and brushes, in case he should be seized with the impulse to dive right in with the oils, Alex reflected that Corey could do a lot worse for himself than to hook up permanently with Wannamaker. In fact, knowing Corey, Alex was convinced he probably *would* end up doing a lot worse.

Charles was older, true, but he was a heck of a nice guy. Moreover, he was devoted to Corey and spoiled him shamelessly. Every time Corey was forced to bunk with Charles for a few days, he always left with a complete wardrobe of expensive clothing, most of which he would either forget about and leave at some trick's apartment or return to the store when he needed the cash. Charles's ability to make money hand over fist, when combined with Corey's ability to spend it just as quickly, struck Alex as an ideal relationship. But Corey was a complete fool where matters of the heart—or the bedroom—were concerned. He simply couldn't get past the fact that while Charles Wannamaker had a damned nice body honed by a membership at the city's most exclusive private health club and assisted by a discreet surgeon or two, he was probably on the far side of sixty. Frankly, were he not already happily married to Tony and fairly wealthy as a result of his fame as an artist, Alex wouldn't have crossed Charles off his own dance card so quickly.

As he continued setting up, he idly thought about what trying to make a life for himself with someone like Charles Wannamaker might be like and, without really noticing what he was doing, he began to compare it with his and Tony's life together. He'd probably end up doing even more traveling, and though Tony's job got them some amazing deals on vacation packages, with Charles, it would be five-star hotels all the way. He wouldn't have to work—not that he really needed to anyway. Painting was more of a compulsion than a necessity for survival. But he couldn't picture the two of them sunning themselves together on the deck of a cruise ship without provoking snickers or smug smiles from passers-by who would naturally assume the May/December relationship was one of convenience. Nor could he imagine experiencing that flush of pride, that warm glow of *rightness* he felt whenever he and Tony were together, the sensation that he and his lover were a pair of living and breathing companion works of art, each different in so very many ways, yet as a whole entity, complementing each other so the sum was ever so much greater than the separate parts.

Charles would be doting, lavishing attention on him, surprising him with costly little trinkets, and no matter how much they might grow to love each other, he would be incapable of eagerly showing off his much younger partner to his dry and humorless investment banker buddies at tiresome dinner meetings or at get-togethers at the hoity-toity private men's clubs where Charles's family had held memberships for generations. There would be gifts of late-model cars and expensive jewelry, a house crammed full of antiques, maybe even the occasional practically priceless work of art should Charles be sensitive enough to the kind of thing that would *truly* make Alex happy. But eventually, and in spite of his own success, Alex would end up feeling cheap, like a kept boy, and he would come to resent it.

With Tony, on the other hand, there had always been a sense of the journey. They were like two intrepid explorers, standing shoulder to shoulder with identical goals and dreams held in their deepest hearts, ready to face life, to seize the wonders it had to offer with all the gusto they could summon, always together. One soul in two bodies, as Alex sometimes romantically liked to think of it, perfectly meshed and loving each other for all time.

But Tony was lost to him. At least for the present and, Alex feared in spite of Joey's reassurances, possibly for the foreseeable future. Charles, on the other hand, was available and, should Alex show the slightest interest, very probably willing. And yet…

With a start of ashamed guilt, Alex realized the path his thoughts had been traveling down and angrily shook his head to banish them. Physical infidelity to Tony was one thing. They'd both "strayed" from time to time and, of course, Alex's occasional sex with Corey was a tolerated dalliance. Thinking about an actual *life* with someone else, however casually, was unacceptable. Alex felt like he'd been on the brink of committing the worst sort of betrayal. Furious at himself, he turned his attention back to his work.

He'd picked Capricorn for several reasons. He'd long fancied doing something vaguely mythological and Alex's painting, like the statue which inspired it, would feature the Goat as the half-goat, half-fish creature of legend. Second, there was an odd combination of sleekness and roughness to the sculpture. The impossibly long and curved scaly tail seemed almost to glisten with slick seawater; the dense hair at the groin and visible underneath the single raised arm and the sharply pointed beard provided a stark contrast which somehow meshed with the lean-muscled young man's fishy attributes even though it gave the sense of verdant farmlands and open fields rather than of the depths of the uncharted seas. There was an elusive quality which Alex hadn't quite digested yet, a notion of opposites combined into one which appealed to him. He hoped to explore it with spatula and brushes and, by that exploration, to eventually understand it and to absorb the feelings it evoked.

There was also the bizarre physicality of the creature. Attractive though it might be—almost breathtakingly so, Alex admitted—the thought of intimacy with such an odd being filled him with mild distress. He could imagine the sensation of his lower body wrapped up and slowly squeezed by the vaguely serpentine tail, his torso gashed where the cloven hooves which stood in the stead of Capricorn's hands raking his tender flesh. And there was something in the face, in the expression, which made the artist uneasy—and it wasn't just the tiny horns protruding from the forehead. It reminded him of wood block prints he'd seen on the pages of some rare books he'd used for research on one of the early paintings he'd done back in college.

The image had been of a giant devil, very probably intended to be Satan himself, a huge oppressive bare-chested figure with the legs and feet of a goat, glaring with evil intent and looming over the tortured bodies of his worshipful subjects. Gathered around his hooves were dozens of naked people, all in various stages of torment, plagued by the terrible violent lusts of the devil-creatures tiny demon minions, who capered wildly whilst roasting children on spits over blazing hot flames. In one corner of the picture, a greenish demon with a long spiky tongue performed cunnilingus on a bound woman whose breasts were partially ripped away by a cat-eyed monster wielding a pair of sharp pincers. In another tableau, a white-bearded man with a loincloth-clad body of impossibly youthful musculature was spread-eagled and chained to a revolving wheel while a group of tiny imps sliced into his agonized flesh with pointed knives and flogged him mercilessly with knotted flails.

The master himself stood center. In each hand he'd held several people, squeezing them in his black claws like ripe fruit, their eyes bulging in a way that would have been comical had not the artist seen fit to include the details of their mangled innards dripping from the demon's fists.

By far, the part of the image which had made the greatest impression on a younger Alex had been the thing's penis—and what it was doing with it. The organ was a scaled monstrosity rendered in shades of sickly orange-reds and nauseating yellows, a slender whip of a thing looking more like a snake's tongue than a male organ, forked and split into two at the end. Impaled upon each barb, hellbound twins in torment, were a man and a woman, both young, both naked and both with exquisitely beautiful bodies. Anyone looking at the picture would immediately know that each of the victims had been penetrated through the ass, their expressions clearly showing the torture of the fire blossoming in their bowels as the vile monstrosity filled their insides with its molten spuge.

Alex felt no similar cruelty emanating from Capricorn. There was nothing evil or malicious about the sculpture, no hint of sadistic enjoyment. Rather, he sensed a kind of quiet and reassuring determination, a comforting notion that were a problem placed in Capricorn's capable hands—or hooves, rather—it would be solved, that all troublesome obstacles would be overcome with a minimum of fuss and the result would be the comfort of protective safety. Above all, one could *trust* the Capricorn of the sculpture. The Goat had a noble sense of integrity and would never do a friend—or a lover—any ill.

As for this particular Zodiac Man's penis, it was anything but barbed. Straight and strong, it thrust nobly from the point where scales met hair, of normal girth if a trifle longish, and with a slight upturn at the tip. The head was plump, the sort of dick you could take into your mouth straight on and suck while still managing to tease the sensitive skin underneath with your tongue. Alex had sucked his fair share of those kinds of dicks many times before meeting Tony—though, he was forced to admit, none had been quite so perfectly in proportion with the body attached to it.

No, there was nothing ominous about Capricorn at all. There was nothing to fear. Nevertheless, looking at the marble statute, Alex could not completely shake the devil image of his past from his mind.

He quickly sketched the outlines of the piece, his pencil

flashing across the canvas as if guided by someone else's invisible hand. The slope of the Goat's smooth back, drawn in three-quarter profile, merged seamlessly with the pylons of muscle of the tail, which strained against the scaly skin. Alex had chosen to depict him in mid-ocean, the torso emerging gloriously from the foamy sea from a point just below the navel where the first faint hints of fish scales could be seen. Most of the Piscean aspects of Capricorn were concealed by the frothy water, but slightly to one side, the last few feet of the tail burst free of the surface, proud and strong.

Eventually, once he started working with the oils, Alex wanted to capture a glistening quality as if the moonlight shining from above imparted an ethereal life energy to the tail, as if the nooks and crannies between each scale were inhabited by colonies of luminescent bacteria transported from an undersea cave, bathing the tail in their otherworldly light. The rivulets of water draining from the scales to reunite with the sea would be rendered in the trademark Restin detail, as would some of the furling wave caps.

For the most part, the scene was one of violent turmoil, with distant waves crashing against their neighbors in an abandoned display of primal energy, showing Nature's inexorable might. A storm raged across the night sky and the stars were obscured by the distant glow of lightning bolts, never actually seen but for their reflection seeping through the roiling clouds. The roughness of the sea, the passionate wildness of the skies, the color choices of deep purples and sharp blues—Alex hoped all would work toward making the viewer gasp at the raw power of the environment he had crafted. It was intended to be a terrifying scene, sparking awe and dumbstruck majesty, a fear of being taken captive by the savage frenzy of the open ocean, to be dragged down to the depths to leave nothing on the surface to show that anything had ever existed there.

For contrast and, hopefully, in resolution of the conflicting emotions he felt about his subject, Alex placed Capricorn at the center of the maelstrom, confident and commanding, an aura of peace and tranquility originating from him and sweeping slowly out across the turbulent waters, soothing their angst, rendering the boiling whitecaps into a smooth, glossy sheet of calm.

First with pencil, then impatiently as he warmed to the passion of his subject, with brushes hastily plunged into the globs of oil he crushed out onto his palette, Alex worked in a fever of creativity. With broad, fuzzy-edged strokes of the brush he created the impression of the Goat's torso, lean and powerful. The tiny, taut buttons of nipples and the curly wisps of down on the chest and the thicker thatch of the armpits and upper part of the groin were merely suggested, as if Capricorn had burst forth from the depths of the ocean trailing hanks of seaweed attached to his body where mere mortals would have mundane hair. It was the beast's navel which Alex felt compelled to render with exquisite precision. A knob of curled and knotted flesh, it would protrude from the planes of suggested muscle of the abdomen, drawing the viewer's eye inevitably to its erotic beauty. He wanted those who saw this creation to feel their mouths grow moist at the prospect, however impossible, of tracing the curves of the belly button with their tongues, to throb with the desire to suckle at the hard nubbin while their hands moved across the barely perceptible ridges of Capricorn's flexed stomach.

With increasing frenzy, he painted. Each daub of glistening paint added to the canvas matched a drop of sweat flung from Alex's brow or trickling down his naked side when he moved to attack a new area of the canvas to try to ease the cramps in his arm and shoulder. His hands ached. He forced himself to keep them limber so he could wield the brushes deftly to create the painting's finer details. Yet as the power of the piece infused his being, he found his movements growing wider and more forceful. He painted with his shoulders and back, with the muscles of his thighs and ass, as much as he did with the almost infinitesimal movements of his wrists and fingers. He reached forward and upward, feeling the play of muscle in his lats as he stretched to add the silvery highlights of the moon, to suggest the cavernous recesses of its craters with charcoal gray and cobalt blue, to coax the peaks of its mountains into being with the startlingly pure white of zinc, his shoulders tightening and his lower back almost in spasms before he was satisfied that the image on the canvas mirrored what he had seen in his mind.

When finished with the moon, he squatted, trying not to slip on the sweat-drenched marble floor where he stood, to focus his attention on the sea itself. His penis, rock hard, dangled like a club between his legs and his balls hung loosely in their sac, but Alex was used to this. It was the creative process, as well as the spectacular alien beauty of this subject, which turned him on.

He surprised himself by choosing pinks, peaches and other warm, fleshy tones as highlights for the vicious waters and discovered the wave caps and sprays cried out to his artist's soul to be tinged with robin's egg blue and mint greens. His brush brought the ocean to vibrant life, and yet it was dwarfed by the placid vitality of the creature, caught halfway between land and sea, that was the painting's central focus.

On and on Alex worked, driven, so absorbed in creation he barely noticed when the handle of a brush snapped from the tension with which he held it. It was if each brush stroke, each slash of the palette knife, were predestined to be perfect at the first try. Often, Alex stressed over getting the glint of light just so or from the effort of making certain the perspective was exactly as he wanted it. But with this painting, in spite of the agonizing cramps and soreness of his muscles, there was a growing sense of fulfillment, a feeling of satisfied completion while he was *still* in the process of creating, something he had never experienced before until a work was done.

Hours passed. His mouth grew dry as the moisture leached from his body to accumulate in pools of his perspiration on the floor. His eyes blurred at times from the effort of his concentration and he blinked them repeatedly to restore his vision, unable to stop to even douse his head with cooling water or to slurp it up from the tap as the prospect of pausing even to walk the few yards to the kitchen to fetch a glass was virtually unthinkable.

By dawn, he was finished. He stepped back to peer at what he had wrought through burning, grit-filled eyes. Like most painters, he often found himself overly critical of his work, but this time, he could see no flaws. The image in his mind had been faithfully summoned from the blank canvas just as he had seen it, as he had known it would be. It was, he admitted to himself, his first true masterpiece.

With that thought, exhaustion took hold and he slumped to the floor. The marble was still damp, but rather than being uncomfortable, the coolness eased his feverish flesh. He fought to keep his eyes open to prolong looking at the painting for just a few more seconds, but his overextended body had other ideas. His eyelids closed, as if weighted by sheets of heavy lead and, immediately, unconsciousness overtook him.

That afternoon, when he awoke stiff and sore from his exertions and having slept on the cold floor, he would recall a whimsy which had seemed so real in the seconds before he passed out. It had only been for an instant, but just as his eyes closed, he imagined Capricorn was smiling fondly down at him—though he had drawn him with a more serene expression—and could have sworn he had seen the man's tail twitch.

Even stranger, he recalled an impression emanating from the painting. There was a great sorrow, and it had to do with Tony. And yet, emerging through the grief, there was a reassurance. Though he would doubt it many times in the days to come, for those brief seconds Alex knew—he *knew*—whatever the future held in store for his lover, somehow and in some unexpected and unascertainable way, everything would work out the way it was supposed to.

CHAPTER 7

"**H**oly Mother of..."

Nadine was, for the first time since Alex had known her, almost speechless. The older woman reached out her hand as if to touch the canvas and stopped, scant inches from the still tacky varnish, and drew it back.

"Jeez, Louise," she breathed. "It's...it's..." She gave up trying to express her opinion, taking it in with an expression of awe.

Even Corey, normally not at all sensitive to art, was at a loss for words, gaping at the revealed splendor of *Capricorn Emergent*. He wore a pair of beige slacks which probably cost as much as a week's rent on the gallery space, with a deep midnight blue silk shirt, open to midway down his chest, the muscles of his pecs and shoulders clearly evident beneath the sleek material. Alex couldn't help noticing how nicely the color set off his complexion, highlighting the darker auburn and russet tones and forcing the brassier reds and starker sun-tinged yellows into repose. Corey looked a little pale and some tiny lines had made their appearance at the corners of his eyes. Doubtless, Charles Wannamaker had kept him awake all night and well into the morning and, though Corey was nothing if not a night owl, he usually restrained himself to a few hours of strenuous sex starting around one in the morning, just before the clubs closed, and was usually asleep by four. Charles, on the other hand, Alex knew to be an early riser and an inveterate napper and had many years of cross-time zone travel under his belt. He'd also recently discovered the benefits of Viagra. Charles would be tired, of course, but Corey must be exhausted.

Corey had always been an amazingly good-looking guy, not only because of his physical gifts, but also due to his youthful exuberance and devil-may-care attitude towards almost everything. When Corey entered a room, even if his face had been swaddled in rags and his body hidden beneath layers of frumpy sweaters, his inherent energy alone was a bright beacon sufficient to cause heads to turn. But now with his fatigue showing, however slightly, Alex suddenly saw how he would age and was shocked to realize that if in the blush of youth, Corey was beautiful, as he grew older, he would become shockingly stunning.

Alex turned his attention to the banker and was not surprised to see him perfectly tailored as always—though if Alex looked closer, he could see a slight smile of surfeited satisfaction whispering around the corners of his mouth, as if he were subconsciously trying not to break out with a boyish grin of pleasure. From the moment he and Corey had arrived at the gallery in response to Nadine's call, he'd been drinking the younger man in with his eyes, mentally undressing him and, Alex was willing to bet, eager to try out more tricks from his sixty-plus years repertoire of sex, desperate to impress Corey and convince him to stay this time.

The artist had stubbornly refused to reveal his latest work until both his best friend and his most ardent collector had arrived. Nadine had railed and raged against deaf ears but he had refused to give in. She'd paced the full length of the gallery while waiting for Corey and Charles until Alex imagined he could see grooves worn into the tile floor from the tromping of her heels.

When the little bell over the door tinkled, signifying that everyone Alex required was finally present, he breathed a sigh of relief. Had Corey convinced Charles to detour for breakfast and a few Bloody Marys, it might have been late afternoon by the time they showed up and Nadine might have been quite literally frothing at the mouth with frustration.

Perhaps the only thing which could have diverted Charles Wannamaker from his temporary lover was the sight of a Restin masterpiece—and *Capricorn Emergent* was truly that. Charles's attention was riveted to the canvas. He seemed to have ceased to breathe for a few moments. In his eyes, Alex saw the usual admiration and adulation he exhibited whenever he was confronted with a major artistic work. But there was also a gleam of something which could only be described as raw, unadulterated lust.

Charles Wannamaker was certainly not the kind of patron who felt that, with enough money, he could possess anything. He was much too grounded and—well, there was no other word for it—too *nice* of a guy for that. Every Restin he had purchased was prominently displayed in his palatial home, not to show it off to visitors or impress them, but merely to allow him to see it easily, to admire it. In fact, there were at least two of Alex's early major works of which Charles was particularly fond, paintings that would be the envy of any contemporary museum, hanging in his dressing room where only he could see them.

Charles was no profligate, throwing money at art because someone had told him it was "good" or particularly expensive. He didn't care about its monetary value. He couldn't give a damn about things like a painting's or sculpture's likelihood of appreciation. Charles knew *Art*—Art that spoke to him; Art that breathed life; Art that transported him from the fast-paced life of currencies and mortgages and commodities into a place where he felt he had come home. It was both one of his most endearing qualities and, Alex suspected, it was also his fatal flaw.

Though Charles was devoted exclusively to Corey, Alex feared eventually he would reluctantly give up on the younger man. Then, aging in a community which prized youth and beauty above everything else, he would undoubtedly give in to practicality. A string of young studs would provide balm to his broken heart and, predictably given Charles's inherently generous nature, the old man would be taken advantage of. It would be a shame.

Sometimes, Alex wanted to just *smack* Corey to get his friend to come to his senses.

"How…?" Charles croaked. He paused to moisten his throat with a chilled mouthful of his favorite Montrachet, which Nadine kept on hand for his visits to the gallery. "How much?"

As floored as she was by *Capricorn Emergent*, as taken as

she was by the import of the piece both upon Alex's career and the world of modern art in general, Nadine was at heart a businesswoman.

"My dear Charles!" she exclaimed with mock surprise. "Talking about price already? That's not at all like you."

"I have never…" Beads of sweat glistened on his forehead and he drained a third of his wine before continuing. "*Never* seen anything so…so…"

"Incredible?" Nadine prompted. Unlike Charles and though she held a passion for art herself, money was *definitely* the gallery owner's bottom line.

"I was going to say religious, actually."

"Religious?" She shot a questioning glance at Alex, who shrugged.

"Spiritual?" Charles sought to describe what he meant. "No…that's not right." He paused to think and came up with, "Soulful."

"Soulful?" Corey, on the other hand, was not one to withhold his opinion on anything. "Are you sure that's what you mean?"

Charles shook his head. "No, I'm not. I don't know if I even have the words to describe how this makes me feel." He touched his dove grey suit jacket with a closed fist in the vicinity of his heart. "It penetrates right here. Down to my soul. There's a feeling of rightness to it. The storm rages in the background. The sea is wild and furious. The viewer knows countless sailors will meet their doom beneath its fury. Yet here, in the center…"

His fingertips reached out as Nadine's had done a few moments earlier. Normally, she would not have worried Charles would make the mistake of actually touching the still damp varnish and marring it with the oils of his skin. But his rapture was so evident, she stepped forward just in case.

She need not have worried. Charles's fingers remained infinitesimally poised in the air above the paint, tracing the line of Capricorn's back.

"There's a sort of calming strength here," he mused. "A sense of security. Perhaps even a kind of competence, maybe? A knowledge that this…this *magnificent* creature will calm the heavens and soothe the seas just by his mere presence. An overcomingness?"

"Wow, Charlie! I never realized you were a poet. I mean, along with your other talents."

To everyone's surprise, not the least of which was Corey's, Charles shushed him with a brusque, "Not now, Corey. Not now." He set his glass on an empty pedestal and leaned forward to examine the painting more closely.

"One can practically smell the ocean, the ozone tang of the electricity in the storm. I love the work you've done so far, Alex, you know that. But *this* is what I'd hoped, what I always *knew* you were capable of. If I don't buy this painting, it will haunt me for the rest of my life."

"Well," Nadine drawled, ever the barracuda sensing prey. "I agree with you completely but, I was sort of thinking. This is a museum piece. I don't know that I *could* set a price which adequately…"

"Don't screw around, Nadine." Charles prided himself on his courtesy, on being the perfect gentleman no matter how nonplussed or angry he was with whomever he was speaking to. For him to cut her off in mid-sentence was shocking. "You'll want an outrageous amount for it and you already know I'll probably pay it."

"Hmmm." Nadine deftly hid any offense at being interrupted. "I suppose we can haggle in the office. *But.*" Her tone hardened. "I'll need to keep it in the gallery until after the exhibition we're planning."

"I wouldn't expect anything else." Charles nodded. "I have a condition to the sale myself, in fact."

Nadine raised her eyebrows. This was highly unusual. The two of them had known each other for decades and bickering over price was not only par for the course, but a part of the process they both enjoyed immensely. Nadine would scream and claim poverty, cajoling and pleading when her tirades fell on his deaf ears, threatening even to destroy the canvas rather than to see it go for a sum so obviously insulting to its true value. Charles would calmly work his way through several glasses of wine, countering her histrionics with more reasonable figures until, at last, they both found themselves happy with the deal.

"I want you to agree," Charles said, "that half the gallery commission will go to the charitable fund we set up this morning to help Alex pay for Tony's care. It was Corey's idea, by the way. Selfishly, it had never occurred to me," he apologized. "That's why we were late getting here."

"You see?" Corey beamed. "I'm not a complete twink, after all."

"Done," Nadine said, without hesitation, startling Charles—who had expected at least a token argument.

"Wait just a damned minute!" Alex exploded. "Tony and I do not need charity."

"It's not charity," Charles hastened to soothe. "I know you're not a poor man, Alex. And Tony makes a fine living himself. But he's been in intensive care for what? Several months now? I know what those corporate health insurance policies are like. There's a cap, which I'm sure Tony's care has already exceeded. Even if Joseph waives his fees entirely and somehow manages to cut corners here and there, there's only so much a physician can do to reduce health care costs. How much longer do you think it will be before the two of you are bankrupted by Tony's illness? Six months? A year?"

Alex's face twisted in anguish.

"I'm not saying Tony will be this way for that long, dear boy. For all anyone knows, he could wake up tomorrow, right? But even then, the medical bills are likely to be staggering. The two of you may be extremely comfortable but, well, I'm quite possibly one of the wealthiest men in this city. Though you *may* be able to manage things on your own, it will be extremely difficult and stressful. For me, on the other hand, while it certainly won't be pocket change, it's easily affordable. Besides, I have already made some calls and have made it clear to certain business associates—art lovers all, by the way—that I expect some *healthy* donations to the cause. After all," he chuckled, "it's deductible. They have no excuse."

There was a long silence, during which even Corey found himself unable to look directly at the artist.

"Charles," Alex finally breathed with heartfelt gratitude. "I don't know how…"

"Then don't. Just accept it as a token of the esteem in which I hold you, and my affection for you. I've never told you this, Alex, but had I ever had sons, I would want them to be you and Tony."

"Not me?" Corey affected mild offense to try to lighten the mood.

Charles fixed him with a stern gaze, belied by the twinkle in his eyes. "You're not suggesting that someone of my social and financial stature would indulge in incest, are you child?"

"*Le Faim!*"

"What?"

Nadine's incongruous proclamation of the name of one of the city's best restaurants took them all off guard.

"If ever there was a reason to celebrate with lunch at *Le Faim*, this is it," she said. "And if I'm gonna donate half my commission to Tony, I might as well go ahead and blow the rest of it on friends too, right? Lunch is on me. Besides, my three o'clock showing cancelled."

"You're kidding." Corey gaped. "You wouldn't lend me forty dollars yesterday and you'll buy me lunch for a couple of hundred today?"

"A couple of...?" Nadine stammered in alarm.

"When he's with me," Charles informed her, "he only drinks good wine. I'll tell you what: If you pick up the meal, I'll take care of the liquor. Trust me, you'll get the better bargain."

"Deal. Lemme get my coat." She darted towards her office. "Alex? You coming?"

The artist had been standing silently, overcome with the emotional outpouring of love from his friends.

"No. If nobody minds, I think I'd really rather be alone for a little while. I don't mean to be rude, but I just..."

"Are you sure, dear boy? You don't seem quite yourself at the moment." Charles placed a hand on his shoulder and squeezed gently.

"Shouldn't be more than an hour or two," Nadine called to him from the doorway once she'd retrieved her coat, her handbag and her pocket calculator—so she could manipulate figures while they were dining. "I'm gonna lock up behind you but you know the security codes, right? There's tea in the cupboard if you need a cup. Do you some good, eh?"

She dashed back and planted a little peck of a kiss on Alex's cheek, pulling away quickly before she embarrassed herself. "And don't you dare *mope!*"

The door closed behind them, followed by the perky beep of the alarm being set. Too quickly, Alex was left alone amidst the sculptures and paintings.

Carefully, he re-draped *Capricorn Emergent,* shifting the cloth so as not to allow it to come into contact with the still drying varnish. His thoughts turned to framing possibilities. Though he usually eschewed so-called "contemporary" frames in favor of more classic styles, or even rustic virgin wood, he felt the Goat might be best complemented by something sleek and modern without embellishment. Chrome or polished silver would be too stark, of course, but maybe burnished platinum? It would add to the effect of the moonlight on the frothy water yet not distract from the central subject.

He dithered about for a while, admiring the work of some of the other artists featured by the Shermer Gallery, scowling at some of the inept talents of a few of them. Although she'd confessed she didn't care for them herself, Nadine insisted on carrying them as her "bread and butter" inventory. Alex was quite taken by one in particular, a charcoal effigy sketched in rough, broad strokes depicting a young man stretched naked and face-down by a rock with one arm out flung over his head, the other hidden beneath his prone body.

It took some time before it dawned on him that his attraction to the drawing was rooted in the boy's resemblance to Tony. The line of the back running from shoulder to waist and the plump swell of the buttocks were upsettingly familiar.

"Turn around," he whispered, imagining the youth actually was Tony. "Turn around and look at me. Tell me you'll come back to me. Tell me how you love me."

As he spoke the final words, a sob was wrenched from deep within his chest. Alex had to master his emotions in order to not throw himself down onto the floor and collapse in mournful tears.

"The worst part," he murmured, "is that I can't hear your voice." His own voice rose with dismay. "It's only been a few months, and yet I can't remember what you *sound* like!"

The urge to cry out, to scream his anger and frustration, to give vent to a tremendous keening of mourning swelled past his ability to stop himself. He opened his mouth and drew in a deep breath, his emotions churning, the sound of his loss ready to echo from the ceiling of the showroom, to bounce from wall to wall, building in intensity like some ultrasonic weapon from a childhood comic book, to lift him with its power and hurl him to the ground, his bones shattered, his muscles torn, his heart squashed flat by his grief.

A sharp slapping sound stopped him; the catharsis remained plugged up in his throat and chest, choking him. Alex turned, already half-expecting some variation on what he would see, put off only by the incongruity of its appearance in the gallery and not among its fellows at home.

The young man who confronted him was subtly different from Alex's recollection of his marble effigy. Though the artist had certainly admired the musculature of the statue, he hadn't expected the materialization to reveal such an unbelievable hardness to the man's body. Had he not already seen such a physique sculpted in stone, Alex would have nonetheless immediately thought of cool, adamantine marble as the only possible medium for capturing the effect.

The statue was nude. Alex certainly knew that. But this vision of quintessential masculinity was not. His impressive torso was bare but for the decoration. It glistened with a sheen, as if he had just returned from a light workout at the gym, though the muscles and the chest did not at all resemble those on the carefully honed bodies of the gym rats who displayed themselves ubiquitously in the city's many bars and clubs. These muscles were carved and strengthened from use, any excess body fat melted by hard practical exercise. Even the man's forearms were taut and compact, slender but firm wrists giving way to a bulge of muscle, the biceps rippling under the warmly tanned skin, the shoulders and chest twitching almost imperceptibly in anticipation of the strenuous exercise to come.

Black leather chaps, supple and worn, clung to the youth's thighs and calves, outlining what was hidden underneath, tightly pressed to the outside of the tops of well-scuffed black leather boots. In one hand, he grasped a worn riding crop and it was this smacking against his leather-encased leg which had created the sound Alex had heard. As he watched, the small whip flicked out again and—crack!—the man slammed it against his thigh in encore.

At the sound's repeat, the stranger's dick, already hard and throbbing and straining to grow even harder than the flesh of it would allow, jumped slightly and, impossibly, swelled ever more. It was dark, as hazelnut brown as the rest of the man's bare skin, the head flushed with blood so it was almost deep copper, a drop of milky white semen already glistening at the tip.

Alex froze, transfixed by what he saw. He still wanted to throw himself to the ground, but this time, he would land at the intruder's feet, to grovel and pray that he would be permitted the indulgence of moving his mouth upwards, to experience the taste and smell of the leather, to feel that single drop of sperm melting on his eager tongue. To roll its salty essence around his mouth, and finally to swallow it and savor it as a meager gift, presaging what was to come.

But he could not move. No matter how much he wanted to kneel at the stranger's feet, to clasp his thighs, to feel his hard, *hard*-muscled ass flexing and pressing against his sweaty palms, to bury his face in that amazing groin and swallow the veritable viper of a dick down to its very root, he could not take his eyes from the man's chest. Alex was frozen with fascination, dumbfounded by the exquisite artistry of the tattoo.

The scorpion was black, deep ebony against the ruddy brown tones of the skin, its chitinous shell rendered in loving and minute detail. This was no port-of-call drawing or head shop creation. It was an exquisite manifestation of artistic genius rendered in flesh and ink, a masterpiece in its own right comparable with Alex's latest creation in oil. The insect's body was located where the swell of Scorpio's lower chest met the chiseled ridges of his upper stomach. As Scorpio breathed, the ink creature's body pulsed in harmony with Scorpio's measured exhalations and seemed about to leap from the center of his chest, to attack with each inhalation. The thing's claws were lifted in defiant aggression, arcing around the outside of the pectoral muscles. The tips—the pincers, Alex supposed they were called—tilted downward, slightly open and giving the appearance of being about to crush each of Scorpio's nipples, to rend them into bloody, torn shreds of flesh. Alex felt a quickening in his groin at the thought; somehow, he knew Scorpio would simply smile during the process, enjoying the self-mutilation.

The tail, with its vicious barb dripping a single drop of poison, the twin to the fluid accumulating at the end of Scorpio's dick, rose in the background of the design. It ran slightly to one side of the crease between the ripped and striated center of the chest, the final curve and the evil-looking tip ending in the deep hollow of the man's throat. As he flexed his muscles, it gave the scorpion the semblance of life. Alex could easily imagine it chittering across some desert floor, pouncing on its hapless prey, injecting vile venom into the helpless belly of some tiny furry creature, paralyzing it and devouring it with violent gusto while the poor animal remained fully conscious of what was happening, yet unable to flee.

"You will never forget…"

Alex started. Not only was he shocked that Scorpio had actually spoken to him, he was amazed at the low, even tones of the man. There was a command to his voice—that fact could not be denied—but there was also a comforting smoothness to the baritone. This man would give orders, to be sure. He would be brutal and harsh, even perhaps sadistic. But he would never go beyond the bounds of reason—or so Alex was beginning desperately to hope.

"You will never forget," Scorpio repeated, his eyes filled with dire purpose, "*my* voice!"

Alex was immediately ashamed of himself. The Scorpion had deftly pierced to the heart of his self-reproach. How could he *not* recall Tony's voice? What kind of an uncaring, unfeeling monster was Alex Restin, a man who could wipe from his mind those whispers of endearment he had taken for granted for so many years? How could he erase the gentle laughter they had shared so often, the late-night conversations they had so relished, the words of love?

Suddenly, Alex knew what a *terrible* person he was.

He had been wallowing in the depths of self-pity, playing the part of the bereaved lover to the hilt, using Tony's insensate condition to verbally work out his own petty neuroses while his partner, the man who loved him unconditionally, was helpless and unable to tell him to cut out the shit and stop whining. He'd been obsessed with his *own* feelings, ignoring what Tony was going through. Alex Restin was a fake, the lowest form of scum, a self-centered asshole who deserved whatever punishment was to be meted out to him.

Scorpio had appeared to him to point out the error of his ways, to drive home to him his stupid, *petty* self-absorptions. And here he had been, fantasizing about having sex with this magnificent overlord. No, Alex was so low he would be lucky if Scorpio would even stoop to allowing him to lick the filthy dust marring the soles of his boots.

The stark white walls and intense overhead lights of the gallery vanished, replaced with blocks of rough-hewn stone, weeping moisture which reflected the muted flickering glow of torches, mounted in iron brackets slightly above eye level. A roaring hearth appeared where Nadine's office should have been. Easily the height of a man, the fireplace was piled high with logs, fiercely ablaze. Even from this distance, Alex could feel the intense heat warming his back and he began to perspire.

He whirled, desperate to escape. Suddenly, the prospect of spending time with cruel Scorpio was anything but attractive. He knew he should be punished for his vileness, for his callous disregard of Tony. Yet, like any wrongdoer, he cringed at the prospect of imminent retribution.

There was nowhere to run. The harsh stone walls revealed no door, not even the suggestion of a barred window. Instead, there were manacles of thickest iron hanging from chains made of impossibly heavy-looking links which were welded to a bracket secured deeply within the stone. The metal was crusted with rust and, unless Alex's eyes deceived him, coated with long-dried blood as well. Hooks dangled from the ceiling, a strappado festooned with dirty lengths of rope which, despite their filthy condition, looked terribly stout.

In one corner, standing upright, a coffin-shaped box was revealed, its lid ajar. Wickedly pointed iron spikes lined the interior, and on the outside cover was a painting of an athletic young man, his torso and thighs showing the bloody results of his confinement in the Iron Maiden, his handsome face twisted in a rictus of excruciating anguish. Next to it sat a wooden horse draped with chains attached to huge rings imbedded in the floor to either side. A dull spike emerged from the center beam, bearing dried traces of who-knew-what. Flesh? Blood? Something even more ghastly? Alex could not fathom its use for a moment, then Scorpio smiled as the artist realized its function. A naked man forced to sit upon it, legs stretched out to the sides and secured by the chains, would have no choice but to writhe and scream as the metal dildo forced its way up through his innards. Worse, Alex saw with horror, there was a pan of burnt charcoal directly underneath; the dildo could be heated to red-hot levels to increase the agony of the victim's torture.

Unable to look any further at the thing, he cast his eyes to the fireplace and was terrified by what he saw. On a stand next to it was a collection of implements: metal prongs and sharp-tipped poles; horrifying constructs with huge screws to be tightened; evil-looking pincers, some with sharp tips and others with wickedly serrated edges; knives and slicers and— even worse, some of them had already been set directly into the flames to heat.

Scorpio threw back his head and laughed at Alex's fright. He motioned with his head for Alex to look at something else and, unable to resist, Alex did.

He could barely gasp. His stomach muscles clenched with fear and he had to force himself to gulp air in order to keep from throwing up. He knew immediately what the contraption was and his bowels clenched at the thought of being subjected to its tortures. But it was no more than he deserved. Justice could only be more perfectly achieved if it had been Tony—poor, sweet Tony who he had thought he loved and would willingly die for but who he had so cavalierly abandoned—turning the winch.

The rack was constructed of rough-hewn timber. Even from this distance, Alex could see the splintery surface of the wood, and he flinched at the thought of the hundreds of sharp particles piercing his tender flesh should he be stretched upon it. It would be like having his naked back abraded with steel wool, he thought, or sandpaper. He shuddered. The huge wooden wheel attached to the side displayed smooth spokes worn smooth by the sweaty palms of the torturers hauling upon it over the years to stretch their victims until sinew parted from bone. His eyes widened as he took in the many notches cut into its circumference, and the wooden stop-block. Any man doomed to experience its workings would be torn apart slowly, scant fractions of an inch at a time.

His balls shriveled at the thought of being lashed to its frame and hearing the clack of the wedge falling into place as the wheel was turned, his shoulders and back screaming with pain as they sought futilely to adjust to the increased pressure. Naked and vulnerable, every sensitive area of his body exposed and helpless, he would be stretched so tightly he could not even writhe as the hot metal tools were brought closer and closer to his tender flesh to scald and rend and tear. His screams would echo from the ceiling, each one wrenched from his chest as the torture implements were applied and he would beg for mercy. Too soon, he would be reduced to nothing but mindless blubbering.

His skin would blister and crisp, his muscles would be shredded, his torso would be streaked with blood and fluid. He would suffer horribly, and through the scarlet mask of pain, he would know that he had brought it all upon himself.

"We should begin."

Alex twisted round to find Scorpio had crept silently up behind him and they stood, practically touching. The crop tucked into one side of the chaps, both of Scorpio's hands were unencumbered. With an unpleasant smile, he grabbed the front of Alex's shirt and wrenched it open. The buttons popped free, baring the artist's chest, and with such power did Scorpio tug, even the seam running down the back ripped open. Alex stood bare-chested; the tattered remnants of his shirt slid down his arms to the floor. The air of the dungeon on his flesh provided no respite from the intense heat from the fireplace. On the contrary, his skin grew flushed and warm, and in the back of his mind, he knew it was from his blood rushing to the surface. He'd read somewhere that torture chambers were often kept unbearably warm to cause such an effect on prisoners; the blood-suffused tissue was more sensitive to pain.

Alex's mouth worked as he fought to cry out, to plead for mercy even before Scorpio began his grisly work. But he was powerless to utter a sound. Scorpio marched him across the floor. Alex's legs grew weak and he sagged, unable to support himself, but the Scorpion simply grabbed him around the chest and dragged him the rest of the way like a sack of old clothes, dumping him on the floor directly underneath the chains hanging from the ceiling. Alex whimpered while his wrists were sealed in iron shackles, the edges digging into his skin, a pale precursor of the pain to come.

Once he was cuffed, his captor hauled on the chain, slowly pulling him to his feet, and when Alex miraculously regained the ability to move and began to struggle, Scorpio lifted him even higher, so his body hung with his toes dangling an inch or so above the floor. Alex's shoulders began to ache immediately; the full weighty burden of his entire body was supported by them. He knew it would only be a short time before his muscles began to cry out in earnest. His upper arms pressed against the side of his head while he hung. He could feel sweat trickling from his armpits and running down his sides already and smell the stench of his own fear.

Scorpio stood back for a moment, seeming to admire Alex's chest and stomach with every muscle displayed in harsh relief by his position. He frowned for a moment, then appeared to have an idea and he smiled again, even more sadistically. His fingers moved between the waistband of Alex's slacks and his skin and took firm hold of his underwear as well. There was a brief burning sensation circling the artist's waist when the pants were also ripped in two. They slid down his legs for his assailant to brusquely kick aside. Then Scorpio knelt and, with a grunt of satisfaction, tugged off Alex's shoes and socks and quickly inserted his feet into a wooden board with two rough-edged holes to trap his ankles. There was a click as Alex's feet were locked into place, spread apart as if he were standing astride in mid-air.

Alex hung in his chains, now completely naked.

Casually, the torturer rolled a wooden stand so it stood with his easy reach. Upon it were a selection of whips and flails and, seeing them, Alex began to struggle anew. He recognized some of the items: whips of various lengths and thickness, stained riding crops, wooden paddles and thin bamboo canes. His mind balked at the thought that some of the things could actually be used on human flesh.

One handle was attached to a half-dozen leather strips with several pieces of jagged metal woven through each of the fronds. Another seemed to be a flail made of rusty barbed wire; a third bore lengths of thin chain and was tipped with what looked like tiny blades removed from a knife. A particularly frightening one glinted in the reflected flames and Alex suspected minute particles of glass had been imbedded in each leather tendril.

While Alex watched, Scorpio made a great show of pawing through his collection, holding each of his toys up to the light so Alex could get a good look at it. Finally, he made his selection and moved to stand behind his helpless victim, bull whip in hand.

The first stroke felt like a red-hot brand had been laid across his bare back. He shrieked and tensed his shoulders as much as he was able in anticipation of the next stroke. It did no good and the second lash was, if possible, even worse than the first. It felt like his skin had been split wide open, the nerves all a-jangle and, with the third impact, he was convinced his muscles and sinew had been severed. The truly awful thing, he thought as the whip fell again, was that no matter what agony he suffered, he knew in his heart of hearts that he *deserved* every lash.

Scorpio flogged him with gusto for a while. Drops of sweat flew from Alex's throbbing body, dampening the stone floor for several feet in every direction. He swung from side to side, twisting and turning while he hung. His tormentor showed no mercy and no particular fondness for any specific area of his body upon which to lay the lash. When he spun around so they were face to face, the whip slammed into his chest, catching him precisely on the nipple, so hard Alex thought the sensitive skin there might have been split in two. The welts across his belly and along his ribs stung at first, but they grew even more tender and inflamed as Scorpio laid into him until having hot coals poured onto his stomach would have been a relief.

As for his ass, well, the pain was virtually unspeakable. Again and again the whip fell. Alex could feel the muscles swell with the abuse; if he survived the torture, he felt certain he would never be able to sit down properly again.

By the time he was finished and tossed aside the whip, Scorpio's magnificent body was almost as sweaty as Alex's. His chest and shoulders gleamed with perspiration, and the copper tones of his skin had taken on an even ruddier glow, as if something within the Scorpion's body was able to drink in the flames from the huge fireplace and reflect them back through his pores. In spite of being nothing but a pulsing, throbbing mass of pain, in spite of feeling like his back and shoulders, chest and insides of his arms, thighs and ass had been flayed to the very bone, Alex's penis twitched at the sight.

His tormentor's dick was fully engorged, the tip purplish with arousal, the head dripping with pre-cum. Languidly, Scorpio ran one hand along its length, teasing another few drops from the end, while with the other hand, he ran his fingers a few times round the large aureole surrounding one nipple framed by the tattooed claws before he viciously pinched it. His smile this time grew slowly, his eyes half-lidded as if he were still in some post-coital, half-dreamy state. He stopped playing with his own dick and removed his hand from his chest, and Alex could see the reddened marks where his fingernails had dug into the skin on either side of the knobby nipple. Scorpio moved to stand before his victim. He drew a small stool to his side and stepped upon it, steadying himself with his hands on the artist's pain-wracked shoulders.

What he did next was excruciating. It caused no pain but the sensation, in such diametric opposition to the torture so recently inflicted, was such that Alex felt he might not be able to bear it.

Starting at Alex's right wrist, he began licking up the sweat, sucking in each drop, his face moving slowly down the arm and into the armpit, accompanied by soft grunts of pleasure. When he was done with the right side, he transferred his attentions to the left and, when finished with that, his tongue started lapping at Alex's chest and downwards across his bruised and swollen belly.

Amazed, Alex saw that in the wake of the Scorpion's mouth, his flesh was miraculously healed. The drops of saliva somehow closed each wound, the ragged and bloody edges knitting together seamlessly, though his skin still remained red and tender. His legs were next and Alex moaned while the tongue lapped at his balls where a glancing blow had struck him once or twice—somehow, his dick had been spared the whip's kiss. When the Scorpion stood behind him and finally focused his attention on Alex's horridly punished shoulders, the artist could feel the ache in his muscles subsiding, the pressure and strain of hanging in his bonds relieved. The healing touch of his tormentor's kiss on his back and buttocks was like a swallow of cool water after a grueling hike across some desert expanse.

The wooden bar holding apart his feet clattered to the floor and his shackles were released. Alex stumbled, unable to stay upright unassisted, and Scorpio supported him, his strong hands gripping Alex's arms, standing so they almost touched, naked chest to naked chest. With unspoken command, Scorpio forced Alex to meet his eyes, to gaze fully into them. Within the dark sienna pupils, Alex could see tiny sparkles of light, but whether they were truly there or just reflections from the roaring fireplace, he could not tell for sure.

"Is there forgiveness?" the creature asked in a low, even tone, not indicating in any way what answer he wanted.

Beyond where they stood, Alex could see the rack awaiting. He had a clear view of the red-hot tools searing in the fireplace flames. He knew he could not stand any more torture. His body would fail, his mind would snap and he would not survive the experience. He longed to tell this unearthly beautiful inquisitor that he had absolved himself of the sin of selfishness, that he had changed his ways and his devotion to Tony would forevermore be selfless and giving with no thoughts to his own needs. He would put aside the paralysis of grief and take action—what it would be, he did not know, but he would do *something*. And his lascivious thoughts toward other men would be cast aside; he would not allow even Corey to tempt him. He searched within himself, desperate to give the response that would spare him more torment.

But, face to face with this glorious man, this agent of repentance, Alex knew he could not lie. No matter what changes he might strive for, he was victim of who he was—of the person he was—as much as he had so recently been victim of the lash. It would take more than a leather whip, no matter how viciously wielded, to cleanse him of what he had done.

Scorpio already knew the answer, without Alex having to speak it. From all outward signs, he affected sorrow, sad reluctance that he would be forced to renew the torture. But the specks of fire in his eyes flared and the artist thought he saw a depraved eagerness in them.

He cried as his wrists and ankles were pinioned to the rack, sobbing and mumbling inarticulate pleas to be spared, his nose running and his breath coming in gasps. Through tear-flooded eyes he could see a full-length mirror, which he had not noticed before, hanging from chains above him. He would be unable to avoid witnessing the destruction about to be visited upon his naked body.

Once he was secured, Scorpio paused to allow him a good, long look in the mirror. The reflection didn't seem to be real somehow. It wasn't Alex Restin bound to the fiendish device. No, it was some other man. His smooth, youthful skin glistened with perspiration and saliva. His toned muscles, not yet stretched to the bursting point, were fully displayed. His face was handsome, even though the sparkling blue of his eyes was muted by pain and fatigue. His hair, once golden and luxuriantly thick, was lank and dull, matted with sweat, the moisture clinging to his body and darkening the thatches of his armpits and groin to a nondescript brown.

Alex waited, unable to do anything else, and gazed up at his own splayed form in terrified fascination. But his captor was not quite ready to begin inflicting pain.

From the rolling cart which held the whips, he took a large earthenware bottle and unstopped it with his teeth, spitting the cork to the floor. He tilted it and a sludgy stream of clear oil oozed out onto his palm. It was warm when Scorpio plopped a dollop onto Alex's chest, eerily soothing considering the atmosphere of the rest of the room. Slowly, with gentle tenderness like that of a lover, Scorpio spread the oil, massaging it into Alex's torso, returning to get more from the bottle when it was absorbed. Soon, Alex's skin could drink in no more and, after Scorpio finished with his arms and legs, his entire body glistened with a thick residue. Seeing himself in the mirror, Alex was surprised at what he beheld. He knew he kept in shape, but the oil coating seemed to add bulk to his slender frame, to accentuate the muscles. Alex had never before realized just how nice a body he had.

His ruminations were interrupted by the creak of rope. Scorpio turned the wheel a single notch, then two, followed by two more. Alex could feel his arms and legs drawn away from the center of his body. There was no pain as yet, merely a mild discomfort and the slight beginning of an ache as he was pinioned to the Scorpion's whim. He tried to move, to release some of the tension starting to build, but his tormentor was an expert and there was no slack at all. He could not imagine a worse torture than the one he was about to endure, but Scorpio quickly corrected *that* error.

Shoulders bunched from the effort, he knelt between Alex's spread legs and fiddled with something beneath the frame of the torture device. There was another creak—of wood against wood this time—and a click as a second frame swung out from beneath and locked into place at the foot of the rack. In the mirror, Alex could clearly see the contraption, but try as he might to figure out its purpose, he had no idea what Scorpio intended to do with it.

His suspense didn't last long.

With sadistic deliberation, Scorpio unwound a long thin

cord from the roller atop the machine. On one side of the roller was a crank. A leather ring hung from the free end of the rope, knotted so it could be tightened. When Scorpio leaned over between Alex's legs, his broad muscled back obscured the view in the mirror and Alex had to look down the length of his own body in order to see what was happening. He realized and began to scream and writhe within the restraints mindlessly, ignoring the extra stress his movements placed onto his stretched shoulders, even before his torturer finished looping the ring around his testicles and yanking it tight.

Two turns of the crank and his balls were pulled out from his body, suspended in midair. Another turn and Alex felt a sharp agony in the pit of his stomach as his poor testicles were tugged harder. A fourth and he feared the sacs would be ripped free of his groin.

He screamed and screamed. The pain was intense, but not yet unbearable. The idea of being emasculated this way was what filled him with terror. Scorpio was not yet finished.

Nausea shot through his groin, into his belly, and settled in his throat. His mind gibbered when Scorpio showed him two small square sheets of thick plastic held together like sandwich bread by four rusty screws, one affixed to each corner. Grinning, Scorpio loosened the screws, and once the clear plastic was separated wide enough, he positioned Alex's balls between the transparent plates. His grin became a veritable leer while he tightened it. The pressure was unbearable and Alex continued to shriek while watching his balls being slowly flattened, able to see each throbbing thickening vein as the sacs were crushed, bulging out to the sides as they sought someplace to go.

Three more cranks of the small winch, some more tightening of the screws and a mighty turn of the main wheel and Alex's tormented body was suspended in the air, several inches above the rough wooden planking of the rack. He was left literally hanging by his balls, screaming in pain until his throat grew so raw he could only manage parched croaks.

Scorpio stood, watching his agony for a long five minutes. Then, unaccountably, he positioned himself where Alex could see him clearly—and stripped. Peeling off the leather chaps was but the work of a few seconds and they slid to the floor. Then he stood, in his splendid nudity, each fantastic inch of his incredible body displayed for Alex to see, and he began to pose. First he flexed his arms above his head, his chest bulging and his shoulder muscles standing out. Then he clenched his chest even further, the pecs assuming even greater proportions, the nipples protruding as if being offered to his victim to bite, to take what little revenge he could by clamping his teeth down on the nubs. But the hedonist was too far away. Next, he brought his legs into play. The cords stood out like corduroy under the bronzed skin and, when he angled his body, Alex dimly saw for the first time that the glory of the Scorpion's perfectly formed, muscled bubble butt exceeded his previously imagined expectations.

By the time he was finished posing, Alex's body was so infused with pain that he could no longer see clearly enough to watch. Somehow, knowing this, Scorpio moved on to the final torment.

His oil-slicked hand closed gently around the shaft of Alex's dick and, through the blur of agony, Alex realized he was somehow, in some inexplicable way given what the rest of his body was being put through, as rock hard as he had ever been in his young life.

"Do you want this?" The Scorpion's voice was so low, Alex had to strain to hear it. "Will it help?"

Through the waves of pain, past his parched and ravaged throat, Alex managed to gasp a single word, "Yes!"

Anything, *anything* to take his mind of the searing waves of agony washing across every fiber of his body.

"Even if it means I will then play with the toys warming in the fire?"

He quirked one eyebrow quizzically as if he truly wanted to know and would be guided by the answer. Alex dreaded what use the hot pinchers and clamps would be put to. His flesh cringed at the thought of being seared by them. His stomach would contract from the heat of the irons, drawing in upon itself until he could exhale no more. Then, when his body contained not even enough breath to scream, Scorpio would press the tool down.

Through vision blurred by the sweat dripping into his eyes, he saw the mirror above his pinioned frame and imagined what his gym-toned body would look like when Scorpio was finished with his grisly work. His chest and belly would be blistered and scarred where hot irons were laid upon them, his nipples would be torn and shredded into bloody pulp by the jagged teeth of the pincers, his thighs would bear deep cauterized gashes from the hot knives. His plump, round testicles, even now feeling like they could bear no more of the Scorpion's sting, would be roasted slowly until they were small, hard, blackened husks. As for his dick, still stiff in spite of the agony ripping through him, Alex could envision a gaping shredded hole of torn flesh where his treacherous penis, Tony's betrayer, had so recently and proudly stood at attention. He lacked the words to describe or the thoughts to conceive what the process of destroying his body would feel like and knew only that he had brought this upon himself.

Nevertheless, the hot irons lay in the future and he could not stand his present torment without some spate of release. Maybe, by some miracle, if he encouraged Scorpio to work his dick, the agony of the scalding metal would be delayed, and somehow he might buy himself enough time to wake up from this nightmare, to somehow be rescued, to be in some way spared.

Scorpio stood, waiting patiently for Alex's answer, his oiled hand sliding casually along the shaft of the artist's pulsing dick.

"Yes!" The word exploded from his throat in a graveled tone.

Scorpio's expression barely changed when he increased the motion of his hand, moving his palm up and down the underside of Alex's dick, his fingers running in ever-decreasing circles around the head, passing for an excruciating instant over the hole in the tip to tease, always returning to his stroking of the thickening length. As his arousal grew, Alex's pain receded slightly, the endorphins inuring his nerves to a small measure of the torture.

"Open your eyes," the sadistic tormentor demanded, and Alex dared not resist the order.

Scorpio loomed above him, looking fully into his face as if

seeking to discover something there. The flickers of light Alex had noticed in his pupils had grown, eclipsing the dark brown irises as if the glowing embers of the creature's soul had burst into scarlet flame while he worked on his kidnapped subject.

Alex's hips bucked involuntarily as he neared climax, each thrust sending splinters of agony through the overtaxed muscles of his shoulders and thighs, every motion causing stabbing pain where his ball sac met his groin, his suspended testicles tugged viciously by the tiniest movement. Sadly for Alex's poor body, Scorpio seemed a master of cum control, bringing him to the brink of ejaculation time and time again while he twitched and writhed in midair, only to slow his tempo, to draw back upon his teasing until the urge to shoot faded and Alex's misery began to reassert itself. Then he would slowly arouse his victim, bringing him to the very edge of the precipice again.

Alex's wrists and ankles where the rope was tightly wound were rubbed raw. He imagined he could feel blood seeping from his abraded flesh. His balls tingled like they were being stung by fire ants as he thrashed against the cords binding them. At times, he feared the frantic twisting of his body would tear them clear away. He felt a gathering in his testicles, one that could be halted no more. His sphincter widened and he gasped. He was about to cum and even Scorpio was powerless to stop him.

Scorpio leaned in closer, so close that Alex could smell the heat of his breath like the suffocating scent of overheated bronze, even through the stench of his own body's sweat and blood. He spoke as if imparting some great wisdom.

"In pain, no matter if caused by ourselves or by someone else, there is often release."

Before the words had ceased echoing off the chamber's stone walls, Alex found he could hold back no more. His dick spasmed with a mighty pulse and a veritable fountain of sperm shot forth. The first thick gob sailed through the air, splashing across Scorpio's rippling chest muscles. The Scorpion shifted his stance slightly and the second ejaculation, amazingly as violent as the first, mounted higher and higher, so powerfully propelled that it splattered against the overhead mirror, drops sliding back down onto Scorpio's back and Alex's chest a moment later.

The rest of the spew was less impressive; Alex's body simply lacked the reserves of cum to maintain it. Still, it shot out in ever-decreasing volume, covering his thighs and belly with its thick, hot fluid, running down his sides and dripping onto the splintered wood of the rack's bed until finally only a thick ooze flowed from the tip of his dick, over Scorpio's hand and down along the shaft to pool in the matted blond hair of his crotch.

"And now." It was clear he was not going to give his subject even a few seconds' respite before resuming. "We continue. That is what you want, isn't it? What you *need*?"

In the aftermath of cumming, Alex's body was even more sensitive. His heightened nerves would render the tortures to come even more excruciating. He could do nothing but moan.

Scorpio withdrew and Alex feared to turn his head to see what the clatter of metal by the fireplace could mean. Sadly, he was not spared the knowledge of what tool had been chosen to be used on him next. Scorpio returned to his side and held the toy above his face where, though he desperately wanted to close his eyes to avoid seeing it, he simply had to look in horrified fascination.

The tips of the pinchers were as sharp as nails and glowing with the red heat of their immersion in the flames. Small, serrated teeth lined the jaws and, when Alex screamed out against the sight, his torturer opened and closed them a few times, enjoying Alex's terrified expression when the captive realized just how much damage they were capable of inflicting. When he was satisfied the artist could not possibly be any more frightened than he was, Scorpio moved the vile implement down, closer to Alex's splayed chest, pausing only an inch or two above it, and opened the jaws. Alex could feel his skin flinch at the intensity of the thing's heat.

Just when Alex had given up any hope of being spared, when he knew he would never survive what was to come, when he had resigned himself to being reduced to nothing but a scorched and savaged quivering wreck of flesh, Scorpio started at the sound of a door slamming against the stone walls. He turned to look and, mercifully, the pinchers retreated several inches. Bleary-eyed and not knowing whether he dared hope for rescue or feared Scorpio was about to be joined by an even more fiendish companion, Alex managed to turn his head toward the new arrival.

CHAPTER 8

He was tall, much taller than Scorpio and his physique, though impressive, was not as obviously muscled. His thighs were thick trunks, encased in elaborately tooled metal greaves; his torso was largely bare though one shoulder was half-covered by some kind of defensive plating held together with leather straps. His groin was uncovered, his dick emerging like a spear pointed at some sexual enemy, long and smooth and thick, the head with a vaguely triangular cant to it, furthering the impression that it was a weapon of flesh. His arms were corded with muscle, the biceps bulging against the steel decorative bands bound around them, the thick wrists straining against the spiked cuffs that encased each forearm to a point just below the elbow.

From the cuffs, a weird decoration emerged, similar to the tattooed claws emblazoned across Scorpio's chest but broader and more substantial-looking than the scorpion's slender, sharp barbs. The sound they made when they clicked together— Alex feared the movement was in anticipation of getting at the tender flesh of his exposed body—was sharp, the clang of metal scraping against metal.

The man's complexion was extraordinarily pale. It would have been downright pasty but for the flush of violent red suffusing every inch of his exposed flesh. It was as if, being naturally light-skinned, he had spent too many hours on the beach or under a sun lamp and had the first flush of a bad burn. He was completely hairless—even his groin showed not a wisp, and his entire body gleamed with a coating of viscous oil which reflected the firelight, shining and bringing the rounded muscles of his chest into greater prominence.

Dazedly, Alex wondered what his face looked like but it was concealed from the bridge of the nose upward, encased by a helmet of tarnished brass or bronze with flaps extending down along the cheeks and pierced by only small slits around the eyes so the warrior's vision would remain unobstructed. The lower part of his face revealed a small beard, cut closely to follow the line of the heavy jaw, and lush, full lips.

One hand rested upon a short sword hanging from his hip. In the other, he casually held a small round shield with the figure of a crab emblazoned on it in bas relief. He scuttled forward with an odd sideways gait and, between the way he moved and the nature of the shield emblem, Alex knew immediately who he was.

Scorpio inclined his head with what seemed to be an indication of respect for an equal at Cancer's approach and moved a few paces back from where Alex hung by the five ropes. A silent exchange passed between the two Zodiac Men, and with another nod, the Scorpion relinquished his prisoner to the Crab.

The sword unsheathed with a soft hiss of sliding steel. With a swift motion, the cord suspending his abused testicles was severed, and though he had thought himself incapable of making any more sounds other than strangled screams, Alex sighed at the blessed relief he felt. Another two snicks followed and the sting of the rack's splinters digging into his buttocks and thighs as he fell down onto it again were as nothing compared to the torment he'd so recently suffered. An instant later, the strain on his shoulders eased as the rope was parted and Alex lay, still splayed out in spread-eagle, relishing the sudden absence of pain.

Chest heaving, he felt a strong hand caressing his sweat-drenched flesh and knew, even without looking, that his wounds were again being healed. He felt the ache in his torn muscles gather in one last shock of agony before it was sucked up by his savior's palms. The spasms eased and a warm glow suffused his being. Even the harsh abrasions where his limbs had been secured ceased to trouble him. When at last he felt once more like a whole man and not just a morass of shredded flesh, he opened his eyes.

Scorpio had vanished. Alex didn't know where he'd gone, nor did he care. He saw only Cancer, looking down on him with eyes filled with tenderness and concern, strangely nurturing emotions emanating from someone who, physically at least, seemed to be such a warlike creature. He flinched when the Crab's arm brushed the end of his abused dick. Cancer's expression softened even further and he took Alex's manhood between both his palms, rubbing and soothing it, massaging in a way so obviously designed to comfort and not to arouse that Alex doubted he could grow hard again even if he still had the physical reserves to make the effort.

The Crab's hands moved over his body, from the soles of his feet to the very top of his head. When he was finished with Alex's front, he lifted him from the torture device with strong, firm arms and carried him like a baby to a table, covered with a soft fleece, which had inexplicably materialized underneath where the manacles used to restrain him for the vicious flogging had hung.

Laying the artist facedown, Cancer continued his ministrations. Alex moaned, for the first time in what seemed like hours, with indescribable pleasure and not from fear or pain. The tension vanished from his back and from the rear of his thighs. When the Crab devoted his attentions to Alex's ass, he was surprised to feel his butt hole begin to twitch with the echo of a sexual arousal he had feared he would never experience again.

Cancer continued to knead and stroke his sore and abused muscles, his gentle fingers ever returning to massage the soft, unprotected rosebud of Alex's ass, sending waves of soothing sensation up his anus, into his stomach and chest, removing the last vestiges of the horrid torture from his supine and now completely relaxed body. He had not felt this safe, this nurtured, since the time a few years ago on his birthday when Tony had confessed that his "late nights at the office" were actually a cover to hide his enrollment in an extension course in erotic massage. Alex's birthday gift was the best surprise he'd ever had—a delicious exploration of the techniques his lover had learned.

Gradually, he began to feel normal again—better than normal. When he felt his full strength return, he rolled over onto his back. Cancer was a gorgeous hunk of man and Alex was eagerly looking forward to repaying the Crab for the rescue. He reached out, gazing deep into Cancer's eyes, his gratitude palpable, and wanting to savor the feel of the swell of his savior's biceps. But his fingers closed on empty air and, with a cry of dismay, he saw the outline of Cancer's form begin to blur and fade. The stone arches of the dungeon retreated, replaced with the modern off-white walls of the Shermer Gallery. The soft table where he lay morphed into one of the thinly padded benches Nadine had installed so her customers could sit down while considering their purchases. The gentle glow of the fireplace was thrust out by the glare of overhead electric light.

Alex stumbled and reached out, his hands clutching at someone's shoulders when his knees went wobbly and he started to collapse to the ground. Arms laced about his waist to prevent him from falling and he heard a voice cry out, a young man's voice, high-pitched with fright. "For God's sake, Charles, call an ambulance! Nadine, call Joey!"

His head lolled and came to rest against someone's chest. He breathed in a fresh, just-washed scent overlaid with a hint of sage and citrus and, somewhere far in the back of his mind, he recognized it as a cologne Corey favored. Alex opened his eyes and his vision cleared enough for him to see his friends, staring at him with various expressions of concern and panic.

"Where..." he mumbled. "Where did he go?"

"You're running a fever, boy-o," Charles told him, trying to be reassuring. He dialed 9-1-1 and spoke commandingly into his cell phone, quickly giving the gallery's address to the operator.

"No!" Alex pushed Corey away and managed to regain his footing, reeling across the floor to stand, back defensively braced against the wall, eyes wild. "They were just here. *Both* of them!"

"Relax, honey. I'll get you some tea." Nadine, with birdlike flutters of her hands, tried to move him back to the bench and force him to sit down.

"No, tea! Nooo!" The last was a wail of angst-filled protest. His eyes darted around the showroom, frantically looking for some sign of the torture chamber, some indication that his beautiful male visitors had not been mere figments of a deranged mind. "They were here," he whispered with quiet intensity. "They did…things."

Charles's level baritone cut through the haze. For an instant, he felt the investment banker's cool palm lingering on his forehead. "You're burning up, Alex. It was delirium." He turned to Nadine. "I told you we shouldn't have left him alone. I *knew* something was wrong just before we left."

"I'm fine." But Alex's protest was belied when he slumped against the wall, and an instant later he found himself sitting, his legs no longer capable of supporting him.

"Do you think," Corey asked hopefully, "…someone might have…?"

Nadine shook her head and pointed toward the camera by the front door.

"Check!" Alex yelled at her. "Check now."

"Just calm down, Alex…"

"I said, *check!*" he shrieked.

With a helpless shrug, the old woman vanished into her office and emerged a moment later. "The cameras automatically take a picture every time the front door opens. Even if the alarm's not set."

"And?" Alex demanded. "They *were* here, weren't they?"

She looked at Charles and Corey uncomfortably, not willing to meet her protégé's eyes.

"Dammit, Nadine! Answer me!"

When she finally summoned the courage to reply, her voice was reluctant, her demeanor lost and helpless, her eyes filled with sorrowful pity.

"There was no one here, Alex. No one at all."

Alex sat on the floor staring up at her for a moment, gaping with stunned disbelief. Then without another word, his eyes rolled up to show their whites and he toppled to one side. By the time he hit the floor, he was out cold.

"I don't know," Joey shook his head. "I just don't know. What are the odds that both of them would come down with some unknown condition?"

"Do you think it's contagious?" Corey was concerned for his best friend, yet at the same time, given their close physical proximity in recent days, it was obvious he was also frightened for himself.

"No," Joey's professional instincts overcame his dislike of the twink and he hurriedly reassured him. "The symptoms are completely different. Whatever the two of them have, I'm certain it's not the same thing. Tony's got some kind of virus. As for Alex…" He spread his hands helplessly. "Nervous collapse was my first thought, but just to be safe, we did a CAT scan and an EEG."

"And?" Charles prompted.

He and Corey had followed the ambulance in Charles's Bentley. They'd offered Nadine a ride but the older woman had an unrelenting terror of hospitals—as much as she loved Tony, her phobia had prevented her from visiting even once. Dozens of Get Well cards filled the counter in Tony's room, all signed with her brash handwriting. The vases of flowers were replaced faster than they could begin to wilt. To make up for her inability to set foot in the hospital, Nadine sent several new, outrageously gaudy bouquets every other day, and even after distributing the excess to other patients and taking the less ostentatious ones home, the nurses were beginning to run out of places to put them.

Corey had called Joey en route and the young doctor was waiting for Alex when the ambulance arrived and took immediate charge of the case. Doctor Caprese pulled every string he could, ordering priorities for every test, and so it was only a matter of a few hours before the results were in. Once it had been determined that whatever Alex had was not contagious, Joey used every iota of his influence to make sure Alex and Tony shared the same room in the ICU.

He'd vanished for a good half-hour, summoned to the chief of staff's office presumably for a dressing down about his insistence that the lovers be together. From the smug and satisfied look he wore when he returned to fill Charles and Corey in on the test results, it was clear he'd won whatever administrative battle he'd fought. The fact that Charles Wannamaker was one of the hospital's major benefactors, having donated most of the money for the pediatric AIDS unit and had established quite a few research grants, certainly helped mitigate any anger at what Joey had done. The calls Charles made to several of his cronies who were on the hospital board of directors while he and Corey were in the waiting room likely helped grease the administrative wheels further.

The doctor sighed now. "There's something going on inside that brain of his. But..." He paused and looked at Charles with angst in his eyes. "Nobody's ever seen anything like it before. His brain's in overdrive—neurons firing like mad. We're completely clueless."

The banker whipped out his cell phone, ignoring the annoyed stares of the nurse and her pointed glance at the sign forbidding their use on the wall behind him. "Who's the best specialist in the country?"

Joey gently reached out and took the cell phone out of the older man's hand. "Sandy Grant in Boston is the finest neurosurgeon I know. He's at a medical conference in Seattle but I managed to get hold of him. That was a minor miracle, I might add, because everybody who knows him knows how he is with cell phones—mostly he loses them all the time. He and I had a...thing awhile back." Joey blushed at the confession and quickly continued, babbling irrelevant details in his panic and helplessness. "I used to kid him that he'd finish an operation one day and hear his phone ringing from inside the patient after he finished suturing. His lover, Mark, and I are pretty close. He uses my guest pass at the gym when he's in town. I got the latest number from him."

"And?"

"Relax, Charles." Corey tried to lighten the mood. "You're starting to sound like a parrot."

It was a mark of Charles's concern for Alex that his only response was an uncharacteristic scowl at Corey.

Joey went on. "Sandy's taking some time to look things over thoroughly. At first glance, he's as baffled as the rest of us. He contacted a colleague—an ex-lover of his—in Europe and faxed him everything to see if he had any idea what was going on. So far, nothing."

"What do you call a medical homosexual daisy chain like that?" Corey wondered aloud. "You guys are all pillars of the community while I was such a tramp. D'you think I could get the president on the phone if I worked a couple of connections?"

"*Was* a tramp?" Joey shot back, annoyed at the attempt at levity.

"I'm thinking about turning over a new leaf." Corey took hold of Charles's arm affectionately and rested his head on the older man's shoulder. "Seeing what's happening with Alex and Tony..." He shuddered. "Let's just say I'm rethinking things."

For a moment, it looked like Charles was going to reprimand Corey for not taking things seriously. But an instant later, Corey's gesture and words seemed to register and the banker's face softened. He put one arm around the younger man's shoulder and hugged him.

"Well, at least maybe something good will come out of all this," Joey grumbled, oddly pleased at the thought Corey might have finally matured enough to settle down, but unwilling to show his pseudo-nemesis how much he approved.

"What *do* you know?" Charles demanded, frustrated and impatient.

Joey gathered his emotions together and reined them in, seeking solace in the comfort of familiar territory. His voice assumed a clinical detachment, albeit one that was frayed at the edges. "These visions he's been complaining about, they're not completely in his mind. There's a physiologic cause, I suspect, though we can't yet pin it down. Fortunately, there's no sign of brain damage and so far, no trace of any virus or bacteria that might be causing it. I've called in a genetic specialist to try to see if there's a congenital condition, but it's going to be tomorrow before she's got enough data to crunch. Physically, aside from the weirdness in his brain, he seems perfectly healthy."

"What about the fever? And the fainting?"

The doctor pondered the questions for a long moment. "I'm not so sure that's directly related to whatever he's got. I'm gonna go out on a limb here, but I'm guessing the fever was more of a reaction to the stress he was going through as a result of the visions and not due to anything organically wrong. As for the collapse, I'm almost willing to bet he was just overcome by everything going on in his mind and his body shut down."

"What about the sex dreams?" Corey asked. "He said they were very vivid. Like they were really happening. He finally told me why he was asking all the questions about some long-haired guy. He said he could have *sworn* we had a three-way! Trust me, from what he was telling me about it, if it had been real, I would have remembered it. Nothing against you, honey." He squeezed Charles's arm to reassure him. "That was before I decided it was time I start looking before…uh…plunging into things, so to speak."

"Hallucinations can seem quite real," Joey assured them. "Especially when they've got a physical cause. The things we experience in real life are, when it comes down to it, nothing more than our brain's interpretation of electro-chemical stimuli triggered by what our body senses from the environment. If Alex's brain is, well, misfiring, it's perfectly natural that he wouldn't be able to distinguish fantasy from reality. His brain is interpreting the impulses exactly the same way."

"Electric?" Corey was alarmed. "You don't mean he'll have to have those things put on his head and get shocked, do you?"

"It's not something we'd consider doing except as a last resort. And you can relax. It's nothing like those old horror movies you're fond of. But there is a risk of accidentally damaging healthy parts of the brain, so we'd be reluctant to try it unless everything else fails."

"When can we see him…them?" Charles wanted to know.

"Now is as good a time as any." Joey shrugged. "I managed to bend the rules even further. Actually, *you* managed to bend 'em, Charles. I think Doctor Grainger was on the verge of firing me for putting the two of them together when he got a call from one of your buddies telling him to back off." He blushed, a little ashamed of himself. "I sort of seized the advantage when I realized what was going on, so restrictions on visiting hours are waived. ICU's on the fifth floor. Go on up and I'll join you in a while."

Fearfully, not knowing what to expect, frightened by imminently seeing one of the most vibrant people they knew reduced to a mindless hulk, Charles and Corey moved off toward the elevators. They held hands as they entered the car. A gentleman in his mid-fifties, whose younger lover had just survived a tricky operation to remove a tumor which was fortunately benign, smiled at the gesture of affection and held the door open for them. Seeing himself and his boyfriend in what he interpreted as Corey and Charles's casual gesture of affection, he was comforted.

Had he been more observant, he would have noticed their knuckles were white and the corners of both their mouths were grim.

CHAPTER 9

Verdant fields surrounded them for almost as far as the eye could see in every direction. Tall grasses waved in the gentle wind, broken up by clumps of heather and flowering gorse. Riots of wildflowers suddenly appeared on either side, vibrant, their blooms in colors that Alex only wished he could duplicate with his brushes and palette knives. Deep cerulean and scarlet so intense he had to narrow his eyes to avoid being blinded. Lemon yellows and startling bursts of violet and orange. Alex knew next to nothing about gardening, but he suspected the hues and tones of these amazing floral surprises were anything but natural.

In the far distance, just at the edge of the horizon, he could see a range of snow-capped mountains, sparkling with crystalline blue, shimmering in the haze where their peaks pierced the summit mists. Above, the sky was a gorgeous conglomeration of salmon and melon, the clouds tinted like Easter eggs from the reflection of the warm sun on their fleecy tendrils.

They rode along atop their magnificent steed, the gentle rhythm of the gallop soothing and kind. With a sigh of blissful contentment, Alex leaned back into the folds of Tony's warm embrace, feeling his lover's bare chest press up against his equally naked back. The sun warmed his shoulders and presumably Tony's as well, as he could smell the familiar sandalwood and fresh olive scent of his lover's perspiration. Tony's arms wrapped around him, holding him tightly and infusing him with the feeling of being protected, though the very idea of any threat penetrating this Eden they were in was laughable.

Alex leaned forward, and Tony's body followed to stroke

the long mane of rich, luxuriant hair that ran down the center of their mount's back. Alex admired the play of the muscles in Tony's shoulders and triceps. The feel of the soft hair between his thighs was vaguely erotic—not coarse or irritating as he would have expected. And the sense of power emanating from the equine haunches, the muscles extending and contracting as the Archer's massive thews ate up the leagues beneath his hooves was enough to cause a pleasant stirring in the artist's loins. He grinned, knowing Tony was sharing his experience. He could feel his lover's aroused dick slapping at the base of his spine with every bounce of the centaur's gait.

Alex buried his face in Sagittarius's mane, relishing the loamy scent of rich sweat, allowing it to combine in his nostrils with Tony-smell and the freshness of his own perspiration. Tony always smelled like he imagined the air of some Italian noble's country cabin would—the residual odor of polished woods combined with the smooth richness of olive oil and the yeasty tang of freshly baked bread wafting in from the kitchen. For his own part, his lover had once told him that *his* sweat was reminiscent of the beach, something Tony called "blond smell," and for the first time, Alex knew what he had meant. He could actually smell himself and he was instantly reminded of the flecks of spray cast off by island surf when the waves rushed in and expired upon the shore. The combination of horse and hearth and sea was intoxicating.

He reached back to pat Tony's thigh, to confirm how in some ineffable way their innermost thoughts, the sensations they were experiencing, were one and the same. Shifting his weight threw him off balance slightly and, laughing, he found his body tilting forward to regain equilibrium, his face pressed against the Archer's flesh where he could not help but actually feel the play of muscles in the beast's shoulders. The bow slung across Sagittarius's back tapped gently against his cheek and he laughed again at the thought that this weapon, so deadly if wielded for its intended purpose, could tickle him so.

Mischievously, he sneaked his arms around to the front of their steed's chest, pausing to tease the nipples slightly before he wound his fingers together at the center of its breast. His chest pressed against the hairy back, and Tony's grip around Alex's waist pulled him forward as well. Embracing, front to back in trio, Alex wondered if by some magical means, he and his lover could merge with the creature they rode and if by doing so, they could become one with the power he felt rushing from his tightly clasped thighs and bubbling up through his torso. The pulse, as they posted to avoid being bounced around on the horse's back like idiots, was dazzlingly sensual. Alex wondered if his dick continued slapping against Sagittarius's back for long enough, whether it would be enough to make him cum. But despite the erotic quality of being naked with the man he loved atop such a magnificent creature, he felt no impulse to stroke himself to climax. At least, not yet. Not when Tony had been returned to him and would eagerly do it for him if only they would reach their destination and could dismount.

The miles passed, fields of flowers vanishing behind them to be replaced with sandy loam yielding clumps of fragrant herbs. The Archer plunged onward, his hooves crushing the tiny buds, leaves and flowers, releasing their scents so that soon they rode enveloped in a cloud of pungent rosemary and sweet lavender, sage and rue, warm poppy and astringent fennel. The land sloped up, the angle gradually increasing until they were climbing into the foothills of the mountain range.

Finally, they crested a hill and passed through a natural gateway of huge rock towering above them on both sides, and came upon a mountain glade complete with a charming lake fed by an impressive and picturesque waterfall.

Waterside, Sagittarius halted, his chest heaving with the effort of his run, bending his forelegs so Alex and Tony could easily dismount. Reluctant to leave their bearer, Alex stood by his side for a moment, fondling the mane, stroking the hairy sweat-flecked coat along his sides. He was able to see their guide from the front at last, and he was not disappointed by the view. Such a marvelous creature they had ridden! Half-man, half-steed, the two disparate species merging in an impossibility of muscle and sinew.

The armored plates of Sagittarius's human stomach seamlessly melted into the powerful chest and forelegs of his equine parts. The groin, Alex was pleased to see, was exactly where it was supposed to be on a normal human being. As for the half-aroused penis jutting out from just about where the human hair stopped and the animal's coat began—well, Alex had used the expression "hung like a horse" before, but until this instant, he'd never known what it could mean. He giggled at the thought of a possible second penis located between the creature's rear legs. No, were Tony not standing right beside him, he would have been more than content with the penis on the Archer that he could see.

At that thought, he turned to face his lover and, the two stood with hands on each other's waists, pausing before drawing closer to relish the moment of joinder that they had for so long been denied. Sagittarius trotted closer and completed the tableau with one arm on each of their shoulders.

Alex took in every aspect of Tony's body, devouring him with his eyes like a sumptuous banquet spread before a man long starved—the hard, flat planes of his chest, which he had explored so many times with his hands and mouth, virtually smooth except for the brown hair in the very center spreading in a Y across Tony's pecs and ringing each nipple with a few dark wisps before descending in an ever-thickening treasure trail across his flat stomach and exploding into the soft forest of his groin. He saw the lean, lithe strength of Tony's thighs, the outlines of bulges in his calves, the exquisite slimness of his feet, so perfect they could have been a geisha's except Tony's were undoubtedly large and masculine.

Alex looked up and saw the deep, deep love in Tony's brown eyes, the smile playing around his lips, the expression saying "I want *you!*" more intensely than words could ever convey. He saw also the fluted column of his neck where Alex had so often nuzzled, the strong arms which had held him for so many years while he drifted off into satisfied sleep.

He angled his gaze to take in Sagittarius with his massive shoulders and deep, broad and hairy chest. His human portions were impressive, almost daunting actually, his arms bulging with muscle developed from maintaining the tension on his frighteningly large bow. He saw the kindness in the creature's eyes, the satisfied smile of accomplishment peeping from the square jaw almost hidden by the short curly beard. Clearly, the Centaur was pleased with himself at having delivered his charges safely.

Like the rest of the Zodiac Men he had met, the Archer was a marvel of physical male perfection. Yet, with eyes drawn back to Tony, Alex knew then no matter how stunning any of them might be, no matter how ideal their physiques, no matter how accomplished their sexual technique, they paled in comparison with his lover.

He was about to move completely into Tony's arms when Sagittarius distracted him by pulling his bow from where it hung across his back. He withdrew an arrow, notched it and swiftly drew back the bowstring, aimed across the lake in the direction of the waterfall and unleashed it. Straight and true it flew, high into the air and came to rest, quivering, its point buried in the sand along the shoreline.

Immediately, the earth around the tip began to churn and swell. Water, clear and crisp, began welling from where the arrow's point pierced the earth. Simmering gently at first, it began to churn and boil and finally spouted from the ground in a cascading fountain of sparkling delight. Higher and higher it surged, the column of spray thickening until it was twice the height of a man. Slowly, the center of the spout darkened as something took shape within it. An opaque form coalesced within the waters and as the blurry outlines became clearer, the fountain's force subsided until it was not much more than water around the creature's feet, bubbling and splashing at his calves.

The man was extraordinarily tall, taller than anyone Alex had ever seen. The top of his head towered above even Sagittarius who, with human torso perched atop the massive horselike body, already dwarfed his two recent riders. His body was long and lean, muscled and undeniably male but with a hint of something softer and more feminine in its curves. The pectorals were toned and rounded but the lines of muscle were not ripped and slashed by countless hours in any gym. The creature's nipples were full and plump like raisins, surrounded by aureoles almost the size of half-dollars. The belly, flat like a slab of stone, did not bear the distinctive washboard pattern so desired by most of the young men Alex knew. It was undeniably sexy and arousing nonetheless, with a hard knot of navel topping the slight swell of the lower abdomen.

And he was completely hairless—the chest and underarms were smooth, pristine flesh. Even the groin was bereft.

The new arrival was unquestionably masculine. In an odd way having nothing to do with his oversized genitalia, he was overtly male. Yet there was an indefinable sense of androgyny about him, an androgyny to which Alex felt disturbingly attracted.

He carried a gigantic earthenware pot, balanced casually on one hip, and from where he stood, Alex could see it was brimming with crisp, virgin water from the fountain. He licked his lips, aching to feel the cool fluid seeping down the back of his throat to quench some inner thirst he had not known he had—to be invigorated by it, to be revived and strengthened by its bounty. For a moment, the artist was distracted, wondering if he had adequate words to describe what the water would taste like before finally giving up and simply allowing his imaginings of what the feel of the water would be like to wash over him.

The man stepped forward, emerging from the fountain and standing on the moist ground. The stride spanned several feet and, amazingly, not a drop of water spilled from the jug. Alex's gaze took in even more.

Though impossibly tall, the body was in perfect proportion— which meant that the cock and balls were huge. Alex had sometimes seen dicks a foot long and, during one memorable college orgy he and Corey took part in, had even wrapped his mouth around a reputed fourteen-incher. Given the man's eight- or nine-foot height, Alex estimated his appendage to be at least a good sixteen inches. The thought of what that monstrous appendage would do to his ass gave him shivers, but whether they were of trepidation or incipient delight, he couldn't have said.

The physique of the man was so impressive, so overbearing in its way, and such an intriguing and arousing combination of masculine and feminine that several long seconds passed before Alex gasped at his dawning realization of the man's most unusual attribute. Though it should have been off-putting, perhaps even repulsive, Alex could find it in himself to do nothing but gape in wonder at the beauty of the oddity.

From head to toe, covering every inch of skin on his gigantic body, Aquarius was a muted cerulean. Even the hair on his head was a deeper blue and his eyes glinted as if the pupils were made of polished Navaho turquoise.

Though the Water-Bearer towered over the two lovers, though it could easily be imagined the strength inherent in his huge body would allow him to casually brush them aside, or to trample over them were they to obstruct his path, the sense of calm permeating the air around him was such that Alex felt no fear. Nevertheless, he shifted his arm from around Tony's waist and placed a hand on his lover's biceps. Was it a gesture of protection should he be mistaken about Aquarius? Or was it simply to show the giant that Tony was *his*, Alex's alone? Alex didn't know, but there were elements of both truths in it.

Aquarius came closer and stopped, standing perhaps a foot before them. Alex had a brief flash of tilting his head forward and playfully licking the tip of the massive man's dick—it was already situated at the perfect height and he would not even have to bend in the slightest to do it. Tony seemed to sense what was going on in his mind and gave his arm a cautionary squeeze, in case Aquarius might object if Alex was tempted to go through with the impulse. Out of the corner of his eye, Alex saw the mischievous grin on his lover's face and knew instantly that Tony had known *exactly* what the temptation had been, and what was more, had shared it.

Aquarius chose that moment to meet each of their eyes in turn, giving them the chance to look into his own, to probe the wonders that lay within those pools of blue-green. The depths of his glance seared, but not with the heat of a fire. It was more like flash-frozen ice sticking to the skin and burning it clear down to the muscle and bone beneath.

The command was silent and both Alex and Tony had already obeyed it before they realized it had been given. They found themselves kneeling before this magnificently strange creature, heads slightly bowed but still able to look up at him to see what he would do next. Aquarius set his urn down upon a nearby rock, then he placed his palm against his clublike penis and, tempting, teasing, slowly wrapped his fingers around it.

Alex heard Sagittarius grunt as if in approval, but when he inclined his head in the Centaur's direction, Alex found he had vanished. He and Tony were alone on their knees at Aquarius's feet and the Water-Bearer's actions quickly consumed his full attention once again before he had any chance to wonder where their mount had gone.

The hand moved up and down the shaft of the length of dick, hardening it until Alex was forced to re-evaluate his earlier estimation of its size. Sixteen inches had been too conservative. The massive staff was at least two feet long with commensurate heft. To describe it as beer-can thick would have been inadequate; the thing's girth was easily that of a liter bottle of pop.

When he was sure he had both their admiring attentions, Aquarius paused in his self-ministration to lift his water pot again, raising it higher and higher until it was poised far above the lovers' heads. With a kindly smile, and giving them enough time to see what he was about to do, he slowly upended it and a stream of water poured out, drenching them, splashing over their heads and shoulders, trickling down their chests, wetting their groins and seeping down the cracks of their asses to pool in a wide puddle around their knees and feet.

The first shock of brutal cold gave way to a feeling of hundreds of tender fingers in each rivulet of water, tickling and massaging Alex's skin. It was an exquisite baptism, so similar to the massage he had experienced under Cancer's healing hands yet so vastly different. Where the Crab's touch had been strong and penetrating, easing his tortured muscles and savaged skin, the Water-Bearer's gift was a tingling, erotic tease. Alex's dick swelled and throbbed until it was as hard as the ceramic pot from which the water flowed. No—it was even harder, as firm and inviolate as the marble from which Aquarius had originally been carved. Alex knew without having to look that Tony's arousal matched his own.

His back arched. He spread his arms from his body slightly, longing to give the water greater access to his skin, relishing the trickles as it dripped from his shoulders and chest to splash his bent legs, gasping as it ran across the upturned soles of his feet and worked its way between his toes, groaning when the gentle torrent made contact with the sensitive skin of his underarms and the backs of his knees. Everywhere the water touched, his senses came alive, his nerves tingled, his dick jerked. His balls contracted, and he feared he would spew without even touching himself. A few seconds later, his body gave up. Instead of striving for the release of orgasm, as he had been unaware he had been doing, Alex relaxed and soon found he could simply ride the waves of physical pleasure, moving with them instead of fighting them or trying to alter their course to his own physical gratification. They lifted him to higher and higher heights of sensuality until it was as if he and Tony were being buoyed up to the clouds on a tsunami of sensual overload. Normally, he would have cum by now—perhaps even more than once—but strangely, he felt no urge to shoot. He wanted the heightening sensations to go on and on and knew that if he could only remain relaxed and accept them for the gifts they were, he could enjoy them forever.

By the time the jar was emptied, long past the point where Alex thought it would have drained dry, his flesh was shivering, partly from the cold and partly from the orgasmic delight. He shifted his knees and moved closer to Tony until the two lovers' shoulders touched. The chilliness was dispelled where flesh met flesh, but the feeling of having been teased to the edge of climax and beyond lingered.

Without giving them the chance to catch their breath, Aquarius resumed stroking his own dick. Quickly, he brought himself to the edge. Alex could see a few drops of sky-blue jism forming at the tip, oozing from the urethra in a presage of what was to come. The Water-Bearer lost himself in masturbation, spreading his feet wide and allowing Alex and Tony to witness the softball-sized testicles, building sperm in their ocean blue sacs, dangling from his crotch. His chest muscles spasmed as he neared orgasm. Suddenly, there was nothing remotely feminine about the massive breast; muscles hidden beneath the strange colored flesh sprang to the fore, highlighting every strand of honed fiber beneath the skin.

Aquarius opened his mouth and moaned as he came, a soft yet powerful sound like the muted roar emanating from a river when it tumbles over rocky falls. Ribbons of sparkling deep blue sperm shot out from his dick, baptizing Alex and Tony anew. The viscous ejaculate, of surprising density as Alex had expected something more watery, splashed against his chest with enough force to rock him backwards on his heels. Where it made contact with his skin, his senses were suddenly jacked up another few notches. It was as if the sensual neurons of his dick were instantly transported to wherever the cum touched him.

He and Tony shot simultaneously; before either of them could grab their own cocks, their bodies were wracked with the orgasms. The only thing preventing them from falling full onto the wet, sandy ground were their touching shoulders, propping them up like tripods. Their streams of sperm were impressive, coating the area in front of them for at least a foot in milky fluid. But next to what was shooting from the end of Aquarius's dick, their combined sperm was like a teacup poured into a lake. For long moments after neither of the lovers could coax out another drop and were teetering, holding each other up to prevent from sprawling flat, quivering as each droplet of blue fluid splashed their naked bodies, Aquarius continued to cum.

Their hair, chests, faces and upper thighs were drenched. Thick gobbets, smelling like fresh meaty mushrooms with a tang of sharpness redolent of watercress dripped from their ears and flowed across the tops of their heads to slide down their backs. Alex heard Tony gasp and wondered why. An instant later, he knew. Aquarius's dripping sperm had found its way down the crack of his ass and when it touched his hole, he felt his ass pucker and release. Though there was nothing physical probing at his asshole, it felt like the biggest, most tender cock he had ever felt was pounding at his rosebud and demanding entry.

By the time Aquarius at last shuddered and the flow ebbed to a few clinging drops releasing their hold on the end of his dick and plummeting to the ground, Alex felt like he'd finished a sexual marathon that had lasted for days. He and Tony turned to each other as one, and their lips met. The taste of his lover's tongue, the scent of his warm breath was, after what they had just gone through and perhaps not surprisingly, very mundane. Nevertheless, Alex would not have traded it for a hundred more experiences like the one they'd just had.

Lovingly, playfully, their tongues intertwined and when they finally broke the clinch and drew back, their expressions were satisfied and yet still held the promise of more to come. Tony grinned and his eyes flicked down to take in Alex's body. Alex threw back his head and laughed. Like Tony, he knew he was covered with thick, blue sticky splotches. They looked like they'd just rolled around naked while squirting each other with tubes of Alex's oil paints.

He reached out and took Tony's hand and they helped each other to their feet. He turned, intending to thank Aquarius for the bounty, and frowned. Like the Archer before him, the Water-Bearer had disappeared. Not even the sparkling fountain remained in memorial to his presence.

Alex didn't let it bother him for long. Still laughing, he pulled Tony into a close embrace and, with little sidesteps, managed to maneuver the two of them to the water's edge. Mischievously, he hooked one foot behind Tony's ankle and they both tumbled into the little lake. It was deeper than Alex had thought, perhaps two or three feet, and both of them ducked underwater. When they came up for air, Tony sputtering and trying his best to present the picture of outrage and failing miserably, their bodies were smeary and the surface of water around them held a sheen of spreading blue.

Alex cupped his hands and brought the cool, crisp water to Tony's chest, gently bathing away the vestiges of Aquarius's sperm. Tony's nipples hardened at the cold, and though he felt neither of them could possibly even *think* about any more sex, Alex buried his face in his lover's chest and nipped playfully at the taut buds. When he was finished with Tony's front, he moved behind him and gently washed away the colorful leavings that remained, pausing to ease imagined tension from his lover's shoulders and neck with firm fingers, running the backs of his hands down the length of Tony's sides and back, allowing his fingers to linger and tickle at the swell of his buttocks where it half emerged from the water.

Once Tony was clean, it was Alex's turn, and the favor was more than repaid. Tingling and sated, they climbed from the lake and lay on the sand by the shore, arms and legs intertwined, with Alex's head on Tony's shoulder. It was peaceful, and safe and, above all, comforting.

Alex felt his eyes start to close as he drifted off into a light doze. He and Tony were back together at last. He wanted never to leave this lakeside oasis. He wanted never to move from this spot, to grow old in the embrace of Tony's arms. Everything was simple. Everything was perfect. Everything was as it *should* be.

But of course, it could not last. So imperceptibly that Alex did not at first notice, Tony's body grew less substantial. When he realized what was happening, Alex rolled over, his eyes widening when he saw his lover's ghostly figure fading; his arm where it was braced on the ground had passed clean through the disembodied chest. With a cry of dismay, he leapt to his feet, then, not knowing what else to do, he flung himself full length atop Tony's body. But his mouth, so eager to kiss those beloved lips, was filled instead with sand that had grown clammy. His chest was abraded by tiny imperfections in the dirt. His clutching fingers were filled with small pebbles and shards of broken shell.

Fists clenched around the bits of lakeside rubble, he threw back his head and wailed his protest to the sky, so recently crystalline blue and now gray and overcast. The only drops of moisture slipping onto his bare chest were his tears. He sobbed and sobbed, feeling like his eyes were rimmed with salt but the sting was worse than physical—it had penetrated to his very soul.

"It is not yet time." A rumbling bass interrupted his grief, filled with a rough kindness and sympathy for his sorrow. "Soon, but not yet."

Through the blur of tears, Alex saw the thick-fingered hand extended to help him up from where he lay. The skin was coarse, the knuckles thick and ridged; even the fingernails were blunted and roughened. Not caring whether this new visitation would subject him to even fouler tortures than Scorpio, would raise him to bliss like Sagittarius had done, or would demand the kind of worship he had given to Leo, the artist reached up and clasped the offered palm, desperate for something, anything, to distract him from his pain.

CHAPTER 10

Given the two most recent Zodiac Men Alex had met, this one looked fairly human though his brow was abnormally thick and heavy over deep-set eyes, his ears were oddly shaped and seemed to move independently of his head, and his impossibly pug nose was pierced with a golden ring. He was an older man, not as old as Charles but perhaps nearing fifty, and his hair was attractively grayed in all the right places. Broad shoulders and deep chest fostered the impression of a squat body that was well-muscled but not gym-toned. Rather, this man had the frame of someone who had spent years laboring, pulling and hauling things, digging perhaps—the body of a construction worker or lumberjack.

The small pointed horns peeping through the iron-gray hair on the sides of his head were unobtrusive and, frankly, Alex might have overlooked them had he not recognized the man and known they would be there.

Had Alex run into him alone, in some dark city alley, he would have been cautious. Despite not being in the least feminine, he was always easily pegged as being gay. He was simply too well kept, too perfectly dressed in spite of the ubiquitous driblet of paint he always overlooked no matter how thoroughly he bathed, too *cosmopolitan* to be anything but a successful and too-obviously wealthy urban homosexual. He would have had fleeting thoughts about the possibility of being bashed, or at least roughed up, by the sort of person he saw standing before him. In a gay section of town, he could see his new visitor striding down the street in an old white T-shirt faded to a dingy cream and a worn leather jacket—not one purchased for show, but one which he threw over his shoulders every day without thought—and blue jeans with the knees worn through from squatting on the ground and not by virtue of some designer name's affectation.

But this man was different. In spite of his looks, the raw roughness that emanated from him and the clear impression that if angered his rage would be devastating, his eyes betrayed the harsh and unyielding image he presented. Orbs of deep, rich burgundy rimmed with chocolate brown pulsed with speckles of an earthen red in their depths. Though they were emphatically *not* human, there was much of humanity within them—a strong and supportive confidence penetrated past the kindly gaze they cast upon Alex, and it solaced him.

Unable to stop him—for the man's strength was prodigious and not to be denied—Alex felt himself drawn into the man's chest, the wiry gray hairs there not unpleasant where they pressed against his cheek, and enfolded in the muscled arms. He felt a rough stroking on the back of his neck, as the coarsened palms patted at his hair. Weak as a puppy, Alex collapsed and, with the fortitude of a massive granite wall, Taurus didn't even bother to brace himself against the artist's full weight when Alex burst into uncontrollable sobs once again.

"Soon," he repeated when it appeared Alex had cried himself out and had started to sniffle.

Alex placed both palms on the Bull's chest and pushed himself back slightly. Desperate for something to take his mind off his angst, he grabbed at what he had known to work for so long in his times of troubles before he and Tony had met. He seized upon the one thing he knew could divert him from thinking, from having to feel, the one thing other than making art which might grant him an emotional catharsis.

"Take me!" he pleaded. "Now! Fuck me. Fuck me hard. Fuck me so I feel nothing but your dick up my ass. *Pound* me until I scream!"

Taurus's arms were unwavering. He held Alex firmly at a distance of several inches from his body and said nothing, looking at him without discernable expression.

"Please, please," Alex begged, whimpering, but Taurus stood mute, waiting expectantly for some additional signal.

"I need…I need *something*," Alex went on. "Something to take away the pain. To distract me from what I'm feeling… here." He brought a clenched fist to his chest and pounded on his breastbone.

Understanding dawned in the older man's eyes, with perhaps a hint of disappointment. When he spoke, his voice was still kindly, but also expressed a certain sadness.

"You need Tony."

"Yes! Yes!" Alex cried out. He shrugged off the Bull's hands and whirled around, his open arms taking in the pastoral glen, the placid water of the lake. "But where is he? Do *you* see him?" He fell to his knees and challenged the sky. "Bring him back to me!" he screamed.

Moments passed.

"No?" he finally said wryly, bitterly, in a voice scarce above a whisper. He met Taurus's gaze once again, this time with determination. "Then I'll take what I can get."

"Soon," Taurus reassured him. "But as I said, not yet. For now, though…"

He knelt and his face was on the same level as Alex's, even though when upright, the artist had been the taller man. Taurus gathered him into his arms and pulled him into his chest once more. Alex sighed, signaling the beginning of some kind of release of emotion, when he felt the coarse chest hairs tickle his eyelids again. His hands roved over the skin of Taurus's shoulders and back as he returned the hug, not expecting to feel the smooth suppleness of the other Zodiac Man and taking what comfort he could from the dry, leathery quality of the older man's flesh.

Taurus drew Alex's face to his and his tongue, when he kissed him, was thick; the surface seemed impregnated with minuscule grains of sand. His breath wasn't sweet like that of the others. It was far from unpleasant, but held disturbing notes of something that had been around for a while, like cut vegetation or turned earth, not rotting exactly—there was nothing putrid or fetid in the taste and smell of the Bull. Rather, it was as if the scent was of something that had simply…endured. It was the smell of age, of experience, of confident acceptance of the way things worked in the world at large, and the strength to take in stride whatever came along.

Alex winced when Taurus bore him to the ground backwards. His position on his knees made it awkward for him to swing his legs out from under him in time to avoid having them snapped off. But Taurus took his time in the motion and with only a little bit of shifting, Alex was able to lie comfortably prone on his back, facing the powerfully built man who supported his own weight on elbows and knees above him.

He closed his eyes and felt the Bull's hands running over his torso, the palms so coarse they stopped just short of being abrasive. The sensation was not entirely comfortable but Alex relished it nonetheless. He gasped when Taurus's hand closed around his dick. It was like the organ was wrapped in something akin to sandpaper though the Bull's hands were substantially softer and not at all irritating. When the older man began stroking him, the feeling was vastly different than any Alex had ever experienced before. This was no gentle gliding of oiled fingertips on the tube of his cock. There was no rough pulling or tugging on his dick. It was a steady thrum of movement, measured and unvarying, up and down, absent of any pretense at technique or attempt to tantalize—a measured and inevitable and practically mechanical movement designed to do nothing but achieve its goal.

Nevertheless, Alex moaned. He'd thought it was impossible for his body to tolerate any more sexual stimulation after what he and Tony had just experienced together, but he was wrong. It might take him a while to reach climax, but he knew he would get there in time. In fact, given the predictability, the constant unaltered pace of Taurus's ministrations to his dick, he fancied he might even be able to calculate exactly when.

As his dick got harder and harder, he absently noticed that the rest of his body still seemed numb. There was no tingling in his chest, no flutter in his stomach, his nipples ached for no touch. His entire being was focused on what was happening to his penis. Silently, he concentrated on his balls, urging them to manufacture more sperm quickly so he could ejaculate and try, try so very desperately, to subsume his sorrow in the throes of an orgasm. He was just reaching the point where ejaculation was imminent when the Bull stopped and, without warning, seized him roughly by his shoulders and flipped him over.

Alex's protest was drowned by a mouthful of gritty sand. He had just gotten himself fully immersed in the steady rhythm of the hand job and the interruption broke his mood. He began to lever himself up with his arms but the wind was knocked out of him when Taurus's strong hand in the center of his back pushed him facedown again.

So consumed by his grief had he been that he had not noticed much about the Bull's penis when he'd first appeared, other than that it seemed large—just like the dicks of the others. But now, with the stalwart head probing at the crack of his ass, he was surprised at his oversight. From the feel of it, the thing must be enormous. Even now, before any real entry had been attempted, Alex's cheeks were spread wide, wider than he'd ever remembered them spread before, separated by the bulk of the head of Taurus's mighty staff.

"Relax," the low voice whispered in his ear. "This was what you wanted."

Alex shook his head back and forth in an emphatic *no*, but he knew it was far too late to change his mind. He would just have to submit to that thick, impossibly thick, cock forcing its way past his sphincter, plunging up the length of his asshole and ripping into the depths of him. Knowing he had only scant seconds to prepare for the penetration, he brought his forearm to his mouth and bit down on it, trying to steel himself against the expected pain.

He screamed into his arm as the tender flesh of his rosebud was shoved aside by the head of the Bull's dick. He clenched his muscles as best he could, but when the pain grew to where he felt as if he would be ripped in two if he didn't give in, he forced his ass to relax. After that, the pain was still there, but more manageable, and Alex prayed Taurus would get on with the act. Hopefully, when the older man's dick began slamming against his prostate, the pleasure he would derive from it would be enough to dull the fire in his poor, poor butt hole.

But Taurus refused to be rushed. First the head went in and, an instant later, it pulled out. Then the motion was repeated, only this time, the Bull's dick went in a tiny bit further. Each time, Alex had a brief second to relish the removal of the wide club from his butt and involuntarily he would tighten the muscles in his ass to no avail. His puny attempts to stop the fucking were effortlessly overcome and he could do nothing but bite harder into his own arm when Taurus forced the ramrod into his hole anew. Two, three, four strokes followed. By this time, Alex figured he was taking a good seven or eight inches and he regretted not having looked more closely at his ravisher's genitalia earlier. He didn't know how much more he could handle, but however long the Bull's dick was, Alex knew he would be unable to withstand very much more without shrieking.

Each movement was slow, constant; there was no variety to the rhythm. By the eighth or ninth stroke, Alex's ass muscles were overtaxed and he could clench them no more. He lay there, his hole gaping, while the Bull grunted and continued pumping.

Finally, the broad head tickled his prostate and, with the next thrust, made fuller contact. Now, instead of biting, Alex used his mouth to gasp. The pleasure born deep within his ass and reaching up into the pit of his stomach was *exactly* what he had needed. He bucked his hips, seeking to meet the Bull's pumping halfway and to help him drive deeper. He needn't have made the effort. With no assistance from the artist, Taurus pushed harder, his dick going in further until Alex feared his prostate would be skewered and Taurus would just keep going until the tip of his dick tore through everything it its way to emerge, bloody and dripping, from his stomach.

Not knowing what else he could do to stop the delicious torment, and not being able to stand much more, Alex focused his attention on the sensations of his own body, consciously forcing himself to come nearer, ever nearer to climax—*willing* it to happen. Finally, he felt the familiar gathering in his balls, the surge, the rush of sperm down his urethra and, with a moan containing much more relief than pleasure, he shot. The trickle was feeble. The surging of his dick lasted only a few seconds—the spasms were brief. Nevertheless, Taurus seemed to know he had cum, and slowly reduced his inexorable pace and shortly thereafter pulled out.

Alex lay wondering if when he stood, he would have blood trickling down the backs of his thighs. He took a few moments to compose himself, to catch his breath, and to examine how he felt. The pain, the *emotional* pain, was still there. But it was muted, manageable. When he finally rolled over onto his back, intending to thank the older man for his kindness, no matter how rough it had been, he saw only the sky, the rocky walls surrounding the glade and the serene surface of the lake.

His grin was wry. He had expected as much.

Then, as he watched, the rocks and stones, the sandy and gritty beach, everything he could see began to waver and dim. At a languid pace it faded to darkness, and soon, even the quiet slosh of the water lapping at the shoreline grew still.

"Holy crap! Did you *see* that?" Corey's expression held one part startled shock and two parts admiration.

"I could hardly miss it," Charles replied, concerned. "Is that supposed to happen?"

The two had been standing by Alex's bedside, frightened and confused by their friend's comatose condition and darting uncomfortable glances at the machines he was hooked to as they hummed and beeped. Dumbfounded, they'd watched the sheet covering the artist slowly rise at the groin, forming a little tent held up by his stiffening cock. There was no further movement until his entire body shuddered briefly, startling them. Then they watched fascinated as a damp patch of sticky fluid seeped through the cotton sheet and Alex's dick slowly deflated.

"Wherever he is," Corey commented dryly while tapping the side of his own head with a finger, "at least we know he's having a good time."

"What? What's going on?" Joey strode through the door, quickly checking the machines that monitored both Tony's and Alex's condition. "Well?" he demanded, clearly expecting an answer and expecting it immediately.

"He…uh…he came," Corey told him, still in awe of what he'd just seen.

"He came where?" Joey obviously misunderstood.

"In his pants, actually. Or he would have if he'd been wearing any."

"What the hell are you talking about?" The doctor was still confused.

Corey sighed with exasperation at Joey's obtuseness. "He shot a load. Popped his wad. Spuged. E-jac-u-lated."

"He did *what?*"

"That isn't normal, is it?" Charles wanted to know.

"Normal," Joey muttered under his breath while he was fussing with one of the medical charts. "He's asking me about normal like I have *any* idea what's going on in the first place."

"Is it usual," Charles repeated, forcing himself to be patient, "for a comatose man to do that?"

"Uh…no," Joey said reluctantly. "I mean, I'm sure it's happened before but…" He rounded on Corey. "He said these sex dreams, these hallucinations, were very vivid, right?"

The redhead nodded. "He was absolutely convinced he and I had a three-way with some guy. It was so real to him that he thought I was putting him on when I said I didn't know what he was talking about."

"I see." Joey stood lost in thought while tapping a pen against the side of his jaw.

"Well?" Charles prompted.

The doctor's attention came back to the room with a start. "The good news is, if he can do *that*, I'm hoping his nervous system isn't damaged by whatever caused this. The tests all look good, but neurology is not an exact science. Not yet."

"And the bad news?" Charles wanted to know.

Joey hesitated. "If this thing, whatever it is…is affecting him mind so strongly that he can, well, you know…"

"Shoot," Corey added helpfully and Joey grimaced with distaste at the crudeness of the remark.

"Whatever. I'm just worried that…"

"Yes?"

"He could be going even deeper into his own mind. So

deep that his body's responding to stimuli that only exist in his imagination. If so…" Real pain filled the doctor's eyes. "If so, he may never come back."

Charles and Corey had only a minute to digest what they were being told. Suddenly, one of the monitors attached to Tony started to buzz loudly and the edges of the screen began to flash scarlet.

"Get out!" Joey yelled at them and the force of his voice and his panicked expression made even Charles obey without hesitation or protest at being spoken to that way.

The couple stumbled to the door, gripping each other's arms for emotional support, and in the doorway they were almost bowled over by two nurses and a technician bursting into the room with a cart holding a frightening array of equipment.

"Just leave!" the doctor shouted at them again. "I'll be out as soon as I can. Now *go!*"

Without further hesitation, Charles and Corey moved out into the waiting area of the ICU to stand, futilely trying to assure each other that everything would be just fine in the end, while more nurses and orderlies came running down the hall and flooding into Tony and Alex's room.

CHAPTER 11

It seemed like years had gone by and yet no time at all had passed before Alex knew who he was again. But that was the extent of his knowledge. The place he stood in was strange and unfamiliar. He had never been here before.

It was a cavern, he supposed, but it was vaster than any cave he'd ever seen depicted on the Nature Channel or in *National Geographic*. He'd heard of places deep underground that were so humongous the roofs overhead could not be seen, of places so expansive that they formed their own atmosphere in the hollows of their cathedral ceilings. He'd never believed it was possible for such things to exist. He'd always thought the description was hyperbole, but he was definitely in such a place now.

A massive plain of ebony rock spread out from his feet in all directions. At a distance of what seemed to be miles away, he could dimly make out a sparkle from the walls rising above his head. He didn't know why, but he got the distinct impression they were made of natural crystal or perhaps some kind of dark glass. There was no obvious source of light, yet Alex could see clearly. The trouble was, except for two massive columns of black stone rising out of the granite perhaps half a football field away, there was nothing for him to look at.

He thought about walking closer to the towers of stone but on second thought, he would spare himself the effort. From his recent experiences, he knew whoever was coming next would come to him. He searched his brain, trying to remember how many of the astrological signs were left. He mentally reviewed the statutes under the eaves of his new home, ticking the ones he'd met off on his fingers. There were Taurus, Sagittarius and Aquarius most recently. He certainly could not forget the cleansing tortures of Scorpio or his rescue by Cancer. Who else? He'd painted Capricorn, so he supposed that counted for something as it was a kind of appearance. There had been sweet, gentle Virgo and the commanding presence of Leo and even, he recalled with a melancholy smile, his odd experience with Pisces of the finned tail followed by his semi-rape by Ares. Finally, of course, he could not forget the Gemini, his personal favorites, though he could not fathom why they would choose to show up in a place as odd as this terrifically large cave. That made eleven, but wasn't there one more?

He pondered the question for a while but, no matter how many times he tallied the others up, his mind drew a blank on the last one. Alex was so absorbed in his mental exercise that he didn't notice the subtle shuddering of the two distant columns until the floor under his feet began to rumble. Looking up curiously, he coughed at the dust which had suddenly filled the air and he had to shield his eyes against tiny pebbles cascading down from far above, flinching as their sharp edges smacked against his shoulders and arms.

His nudity didn't bother him at all. Each time he'd met one of the Zodiac Men, he'd either been naked at the start, or ended up that way. In fact, he was grateful for it as he was sweating heavily like he had a fever and the air of the cave felt cool and soothing where currents washed over his bare skin.

Suddenly, the floor shifted with a loud wrenching sound and he was flung to the ground. Momentarily, his vision was obscured by dust. Frantically scrubbing his eyes, he sought to see what was happening around him. His eyes took things in before his mind managed to comprehend them. His first thought was that the columns had either gotten closer somehow, or that the shifting and tilting of the ground had propelled him in their direction. Then he saw them move and realized that, impossibly, they were not columns at all. They were the feet, ankles and calves of some megalithic being.

He craned his head upwards, tilting farther and farther back until his neck muscles twinged. As the creature came closer, he realized it was not quite so amazingly huge as he'd at first thought. Still, its size was impressive and daunting.

The man soared above him, his head forty, perhaps fifty feet in the air. His nude body was made of immaculate stone— Alex could see the darker veins of the marble in the rock that substituted for pale creamy, human flesh. Had the man been more moderately sized, his physique would have been spectacular, or so Alex assumed. But given his immensity, it was hard for Alex's more salacious instincts to kick in. His dick, of course, had stiffened immediately, but the only conscious thought the artist could muster was a silent plea that *this* goliath of a man would *not* want to fuck him. He would be ripped apart in an instant if not completely crushed, and he stood awestruck and terrified at what might be coming next.

The colossus approached. With each step nearer the ground trembled, and when he was within reach, he stopped and, perhaps taking pity on the Lilliputian before him, dropped to his knees. His face, once it came into view, was unearthly beautiful and, in some indefinable way, completely alien to anything human. The eyes were too narrow with epicanthic folds that were strangely out of proportion; they were not so much Oriental as they were reptilian. The nose was aquiline and entirely too long, and the mouth was much too thin to have such broad lips. The nipples were perfectly formed buds but far too tiny for the aureoles that surrounded them. Even the fingers were odd—long slim digits tapering to oversized and blunt fingernails entirely inappropriate for their slenderness.

The man's dick reminded Alex of the Washington Monument—not only was it much closer to the size of a building than anything which naturally occurred on a man's body, but it seemed more squared off than rounded, though there were no actual angles to be observed. From the base of the penis hung two testicles almost the size of compact cars, each of them supported by the pan of a massive scale which the creature held in one hand.

"Libra," Alex whispered, almost dumbfounded.

The giant nodded and it looked very hard as if he was trying not to smile and not quite able to completely suppress his delight at being recognized.

"The time," he said, "has come."

Contrary to what Alex expected, Libra's voice was not at all resounding or thunderous. Instead, it was a high and clear tenor, reminding Alex of a flute or an oboe played at its higher register. Moreover, the strangeness of the man's form was reflected in his tone. It was expressive, almost merry, but Alex could not quite put his finger on an exact interpretation; there was a frustrating and elusive subtext. Even in a short sentence, the vocal inflections were weird to the ear.

With a grunt and a grimace of mild discomfort, Libra reached down with his free hand and took hold of his right ball. It must have been extraordinarily heavy as his arm muscles bulged with the strain of shifting it off the pan of the scale so it dangled freely between his legs. The right testicle was followed by the left after similar effort. When both huge balls were unsupported and swinging in the cavern's breeze, Alex had to stop himself from taking a step backwards. It would be far too easy for him to be crushed beneath their weight.

Libra lowered the base of the scale to rest on the floor. Then he paused, seemingly waiting for Alex to do something. But the artist was baffled and did not know what was expected of him. Long minutes passed while the two remained still, the only motion the slight movement of the massive brass scales hanging from their chains and swaying in the light wind. Finally, Alex cleared his throat and spread his hands in a gesture of confusion.

Libra's eyes widened and he seemed embarrassed at himself. With a shy smile of apology, he placed a single finger on one of the scale pans and pushed it down until it rested on the floor. Alex took a hesitant step forward and, at a nod of approval from the giant, he took several more. The brass of the weighing instrument was cold on the bare soles of his feet, almost stinging, and his footing was uneven given the slope of the pan. Alex grabbed one of the chains to steady himself and, assuming that Libra would eventually remove his finger and the pan would soar back to its original place, he quickly moved to the center. This way, when the thing was released, at least he was less likely to be tossed out and crash down into a broken mass of bone and shattered flesh on the hard stone floor. He spread his arms and took hold of the chains more firmly to support himself, just in case.

An instant later, he felt his stomach drop as he was airborne. He tightened his grip. He was no longer quite so fearful of falling, but rather exhilarated by the swift lift into the air. He was reluctant to let go of the chain lest he pass out from the heady thrill. Upwards he soared until he was directly in front of Libra's face. The creature's expression was hard to determine, but Alex had the distinct impression he was being examined with avid curiosity. Unconsciously, he straightened his back, squared his shoulders and expanded his chest. He didn't know how he knew it, but he was certain that gaining Libra's approval was crucial to something very important.

A good five minutes passed before the Scale-Bearer eventually smiled—a sweet, satisfied smile as if he were pleased by a job well done.

"Now," his voice rang out in dulcimer tones, "we may begin."

Charles lurched out and grabbed Joey by the biceps as he rushed by, his fingers squeezing so tightly into the muscle that the doctor winced.

"What the devil is going on in there?"

"I told you…" Joey's voice was desperate. "We don't know. Listen, Charles." He began to pry the older man's grip from his arm. "As soon as we know what's causing this…"

"I don't care what's causing it," Charles told him firmly but not unkindly. "I want to know what's happening to him as we speak."

Joey allowed his impatience and irritation to show. "I have to get back in there and…"

"No, you don't," the banker interrupted him again. "I counted four doctors going into that room. And *you*, my friend, look like hell. White as a sheet and terrified, and I want to know why. I love Alex and Tony as much as the rest of you. So, doctor, you are going to settle down, take a deep breath, let me buy you a coffee and tell us what the hell is going on."

"When he's like this," Corey piped in with unaccustomed meekness, "it's better to do what he says."

He had been sitting in one of the chairs in the visitors'

lounge, plucking tissue after tissue from a nearby box and compulsively shredding them into tiny strips of paper. His lap, the arms of the chair and the floor around his feet were littered with the torn scraps.

"Look at me, Joseph, and tell me there's one thing, anything that you can do in there that they can't."

Charles waited for his answer but Joey could not meet his eyes.

"See? Corey, would you please go to the vending machine and get us all coffee? The doctor will take his black. You know how I like mine."

He pulled a handful of change from his pocket and without relinquishing the doctor, handed it to his young lover. Corey's need to know what was happening to his best friend was killing him, but he knew well the mood Charles was in and didn't dare contradict him for fear of starting an argument. He scampered off toward the vending machines across the lounge.

Charles pulled an empty chair up to a little table and guided Joey into it, making sure he was firmly seated before finally letting go of him.

"Well," the doctor began, but Charles held up one hand to silence him.

"Corey will be right back. I want him to hear this too."

From the mild cursing coming from the direction of the vending machines, Corey seemed to be having some trouble. It took several long moments, but eventually he returned to the table with three coffees and some rather tattered-looking granola bars.

"I figured we could all use a little sugar boost right about now," he explained. "And to hell with your diet, Charles. It's medicinal."

Joey opened his mouth to launch his speech, but again Charles stopped him with a warning glare and by pushing the coffee cup across the table towards him.

"Drink," he commanded.

Joey seemed almost surprised to find the cup in front of him. The look of gratitude he gave Charles after the first sip spoke volumes. "God, I needed that."

"No, you need twelve hours of sleep and a two-week vacation. But for the moment, coffee will have to do. Now, please tell us what's happening."

Joey cradled the cup between his hands, relishing the warmth and inhaling the bitter steam. When he spoke, his voice was hushed and timid, like a young child's.

"He died, Charles. Right in front of us he just…died." He saw the alarm on both their faces and hastened to add, "We brought him back, thank God, but it was touch and go. And now, well…" He squirmed in his chair. "His blood pressure's falling and we don't know why. There's *nothing* wrong with him and we still can't stop it. We've got him stable but, just barely. At any moment…" His voice trailed off. "Then, in the middle of everything with Alex…" He choked back a sob.

"Tony?" Charles asked gently and the doctor nodded with silent tears streaming down his cheeks.

"He coded."

At Corey's grunt of confusion, Joey explained. "Tony's heart stopped too. We just shifted the crash cart and got him back, but again…" He pulled the cup to his chest and cradled it there, not seeming to mind the drops of hot liquid that sloshed over the edge and down the front of his white coat. "We're losing them, Charles. We're losing them both."

"That's crazy," Corey blurted out. "A few hours ago Alex was fine and Tony, well, Tony's been the same for weeks and weeks."

Charles patted the back of Joey's hand where it rested on the table. "Doesn't anybody have any idea…?"

"Not a clue. We pulled blood from Tony and rushed it to the lab to see if the virus has gotten more aggressive. Results'll be back within the hour but… oh, Charles. I'm so afraid it's going to be too late."

Then, Doctor Joey Caprese, the man whose picture might well have appeared in the encyclopedia under the heading "tightly wound anal retentive," to everyone's astonishment, thrust the coffee cup away from him, put his head down onto his arms and began to cry with great wracking sobs. Corey immediately got up and, with his own lower lip trembling to hold back tears, stood behind Joey and rubbed at his heaving shoulders. Charles reached out and stroked the doctor's head.

"Just let it out," Charles urged. Joey sniffed a few times, cast about for a tissue and, finding none within reach, uncharacteristically used the arm of his jacket to wipe his eyes and nose.

The three unlikely friends sat for a while, crying with varying degrees of volume until the tears at last ceased flowing. When they were finished, Charles cleared his throat a few times before he was able to speak. "Corey, you'd better call Nadine. And his therapist, what's her name?"

"Cheryl," Joey told him, then to Corey, "It's in the book under Dawn-squirrel. How many of *those* could there be in this city?"

Corey made as if to comply, thankful for something to do to keep him occupied. But before he'd gotten more than a few feet from the table, one of the orderlies poked his head into the lounge and called out, "Doctor Caprese? You'd better go in there."

In a flash, Joey had dashed the remnants of tears from his eyes and bolted off.

"What's wrong?" Charles demanded.

"Um, you'll have to talk to one of the doctors…"

"Young man," Charles cut him off and brought the full might of his impressive personality to bear on the hapless orderly. "I was not *asking*…" His voice held a distinct note of warning in it.

The orderly said nothing. He simply and sadly shook his head.

Alex watched in wonder as little motes of sparkling gold dust appeared on the empty scale opposite from where he stood. The tiny particles glowed as they wound about each other in a pixie-like *pas de deux* which he found delightful to watch. Grinning at first, he followed the tiny dancers weaving in and out. Their motions grew faster and more intricate, and finally Alex found himself laughing with joy at their graceful antics. As the pace increased, so did the illumination they generated until, try as he might to see what they were doing, he had to release his grip from the scale pan's chains to shield his eyes.

Through closed lids he sensed the luminescence abating and opened his eyes. There on the other pan stood his lover, gloriously nude, his bare skin kissed by the fairy-like motes so that it seemed as if Tony's body was generating the glow. Tony was smiling placidly and warmly with an air of complete and utter content. Alex longed to leap the distance between them, to stand beside him and take him in his arms and never to let him go, but he knew the weighing pans were too far apart.

All thoughts of falling fleeing from his mind, he stretched both his arms out in Tony's direction. The scale swayed but his feet were firmly planted. He longed to call out to his lover but found he could not make a sound.

Tony seemed not to see him and Alex felt a hitch in his chest when he realized he was somehow invisible to the man he loved. But the expression on Tony's face was so beatific, so peaceful, Alex feared any sound he might make to call attention to himself might interrupt the ecstatic reverie and, that, he did not want to do. To deny his lover the experience of whatever he was feeling would be selfish, a crime, and Alex wanted nothing more than for Tony to have more of whatever it was.

"We begin."

The artist scarcely heard Libra's voice and only realized he had spoken when the brass under his feet began swaying once again. The strange giant held the scales out from his body, allowing Tony's and Alex's weight to shift the pans. Up and down they moved in a slow seesaw motion. First Alex was lifted up, so far that he dropped to his knees and scurried to the edge, unmindful of the vast drop below, if only he could keep his lover in sight. Then he sat back on his butt, stretching his neck when Tony passed by and ascended above him, desperately seeking to keep him in view until all he could see was the polished brass bottom of the opposing pan.

The arcs were huge at first. Alex felt like he was in a fast-moving elevator. His stomach repeatedly dropped, recovered itself, then dropped again. The air rushing past made him dizzy with exhilaration. All through the back-and-forth motion, he held only one thought in his mind: Tony.

So gradually that it was almost imperceptible, the movement of the scales slowed. The arcs became less distinct and he was able to see Tony throughout the entirety of the swing. After what seemed the longest time, the pans wobbled within a few scant feet of equality, shimmering and swaying until finally, they reached equilibrium.

When it seemed like all motion had stopped, the huge face of Libra came closer and he critically examined the weighing pans. First one, then the other captured his attention. He grunted softly a few times with brow furrowed in concentration. Alex had no idea what he was doing.

Finally, after an interminable time, Libra smiled and spoke. "It is done."

Alex and Tony were in perfect balance.

When Joey Caprese came into the lounge again, he looked both lost and haggard. Wordlessly, he picked up his previously forgotten and now cold cup of coffee and drained it in a few long swallows. His face was pale, his eyes sunken in deep pits. Though the doctor was a handsome young man, Charles and Corey both had their first inklings that he would not age very well.

The couple clutched each other's hands tightly. Their fingers would be stiff and sore tomorrow, but for the moment, neither had any attention to spare for anything other than Joey. They impatiently waited, not daring to speak, for the doctor to give them news—while at the same time, terrified that he would.

"I'm sorry," Joey whispered. He seemed to be speaking only to the empty air. Corey choked back a gasp of denial and the sound seemed to stir Joey's eyes into coming back into focus.

"Who?" Charles began. "I mean…which one?" His voice was dull and leaden with disbelief.

"Both," Joey said. "They're both gone. They died…" His throat dried up and he had to clear it before beginning again. "They died at the same moment."

Tears streamed down Charles's cheeks. Corey's eyes darted around the room, seeking to focus on something, as if his mind had refused to comprehend what he'd just heard. The coffee cup

Joey had been holding hit the floor with a moist plop. Without another word, Joey turned and, staggering like some drunken automaton, he left the room.

CHAPTER 12

"What do you mean, no funeral?" Nadine was furious. "This is Alex Restin we're talking about here! Not some wino who died on the street. I never heard of such a thing!"

Charles Wannamaker shifted his stance uncomfortably. He held his once stylish hat in his hands. Now it was mangled and twisted like a wrung out washcloth.

"There will be a memorial service, of course. I was rather hoping you'd agree to some sort of special showing of his work."

Nadine dismissed the idea as if it had already been taken care of. "Of course," she said. "But what's this nonsense about the funeral?"

"There are no bodies, Nadine," Charles explained patiently again. He'd known this meeting would be terribly difficult and that Nadine would be apoplectic, but it had been almost a week since Alex and Tony had died and he had been unable to think of any more excuses to postpone it.

"How can they lose two bodies? *Two* bodies in the *same* day?"

Charles shrugged. He'd been over this with the hospital several times. When no one could give him a satisfactory answer, his lawyers had revisited it with the hospital's legal staff. No matter how much he threatened, pleaded, no matter how rational he was or how logically he urged them to come up with an answer, none was forthcoming. Alex and Tony had vanished without a trace. No one knew how it had happened and nobody knew where they were. "Joey's a mess about it."

"He *should* be!" the old lady cried.

"I'm serious, Nadine. Corey and I both think he's on the verge of a breakdown. If you see him, I'm warning you to take it easy."

"How could such a thing happen? It's bad enough that

both…" A sob crept out. "That both my boys are gone."

"Here. Use this." Charles handed her a silk pocket square and she looked blankly at the proffered piece of cloth. "Your eye makeup. It's all blotchy." He smiled sadly at her. "We may be a couple of decrepit old codgers, my dear, but there's no reason we have to look like we are."

She snatched the handkerchief and blotted at her eyes so forcefully that Charles feared she would accidentally put one of them out. When she held the cloth out to him to take from her, he indicated she should keep it and, for the rest of the conversation, she tugged at it as if trying to rip it in half.

"After it was…over," he began, "Corey and I went to see them. Joey just couldn't bring himself to go back. They were so… so *peaceful*, Nadine. And they looked so happy. All the color was back in Tony's face—they'd taken the breathing tube out and I swear, he looked as good as he did when he got back from that cruise, just before he took sick. And Alex…" He gulped air to keep from starting to cry again. "Alex had this smile on his face. You know the way he was when he saw a painting he was taken with? It was like at the very moment he passed, he had seen something indescribably beautiful and…and it filled him with…I don't know…bliss.

"We stayed with them for a while. Corey kept arranging and rearranging the sheets for some reason. Just before we left the room, I…" He choked with emotion, unable to continue until he'd mastered it. "I took their hands—they were still quite warm—and I laced them together. I don't know why I did it. It just seemed like the right thing to do. Then there were papers to sign and forms to fill out. Any time someone dies they make you sit down with one of the doctors for a little talk. I suspect they think it eases the grief but, frankly, it's just an irritating nuisance. All Corey and I wanted to do was either go home, or go back in and sit with them. We couldn't seem to make up our minds which was best to do. Normally Joey would have been the one to meet with but…" He shook his head. "I'm worried about him. He always seems so confident."

"Bossy, is what I call him." Nadine said with a meager attempt at smiling through her tears.

"True. But he completely collapsed. He walked around like a zombie, actually banging into the walls without noticing. One of the other doctors had to sedate him. Not very appropriate for a physician in his position, I know. Especially not after he'd just finished going head to head with his boss about putting them in the same room in the ICU. Fortunately," Charles blushed with false modesty, "I'm not without influence. I was able to manage things so he won't lose his job. At the same time, I insisted they give him bereavement leave even though Alex and Tony weren't, strictly speaking, relatives. I hired an extremely attractive young friend of Corey's to be his companion and this morning, we put the two of them on a cruise ship for the next two weeks."

"While I am fascinated by your rousing stories of the young, beautiful, gay and rich, Charles, I'm waiting for you to tell me how the damned hospital *lost* my boys!"

The old gentleman fidgeted uncomfortably. He still hadn't managed to make sense of what had happened and, frankly, he disliked being forced to remember it.

"We were gone for maybe an hour and, when we went back into the room to say one last goodbye..." His words faded and he looked like a kicked puppy.

"They just disappeared?"

"The two nurses at the duty station swore up and down that no one had gone into the room after we left. Besides, it would have been tough for them to miss two bodies being wheeled down the hall. The...um...morgue people hadn't even been called yet. The hospital prefers to do that after the families have left. We double-checked anyway but none of the attendants in the morgue even knew anyone had died, let alone had come up and collected them."

Nadine repressed her urge to launch into a tirade about the incompetence of everyone involved with the situation when she saw how miserable Charles looked. It was an effort to quell her angry grief, but she mastered it.

"I'm sorry, Charles. I don't like this. Not one bit. But I know if there was anything anybody could do to solve this terrible mystery, you've already done it."

"Thank you. I mean that sincerely."

"Well." She made a fairly passable effort to return to her normal attitude of brisk business. "We'll have the memorial here, then. I know a church is traditional but neither of them was particularly devout and besides, *this* was Alex's church."

Charles nodded.

"I'll need to get into the new apartment. I've already got the keys to the townhouse, so all I have to do is let the tenants know when I'm coming over. I'm planning on moving all this other stuff..." She indicated the paintings lining the walls and the sculptures on the various pedestals. "...into temporary storage. I don't want anything in this place for the memorial that isn't Alex's work. When I go over to this library place he bought, I'll need to borrow Corey. If anyone knows where Alex kept things he was working on or pieces he'd finished but hadn't shown me yet, it'd be your boy toy."

"I'm not so sure," Charles began slowly, "we can call him that any more. This whole experience has changed him. Normally he's in and out of my life for only a few days at most, but this time, well, it's been almost two weeks, and do you know the little dickens hasn't even disappeared for a night on the town in the bars? Not once."

"I'm happy for you, Charles." She realized how dull and toneless her voice sounded and quickly forced some life into it. "No, really, I am. It's about time he settled down and I can't think of anyone better than you to rein him in. Besides, I know how you've felt about him for years now and, well, I'd like to say that you deserve the best. Only I'm not sure that Corey *is* the best. Nevertheless, I know how happy he makes you, Charles, and for that, I'm glad. I'm just..." Her shoulders sagged a bit. "Tired, Charles. I'm terribly tired. I don't mean to be rude, but I really think I'd like to be alone."

"Of course." Charles placed his mangled hat on his head and moved toward the door.

"Just make sure to send the new, improved and, please pray God, more mature version of the boy toy over here tomorrow so I can get started planning a memorial showing. There's a lot to do and not a bunch of time, but I guess the activity will do me good."

Charles Wannamaker paused in the doorway and, looking back at the proud capable businesswoman he had known for so many years and seeing how defeated and small she suddenly looked, he sighed. For the first time in a very long time, he felt the burden of every year of his age.

"Well, Charles, I may not be as rich as you are but…"

Corey stood in the center of the condo. His eyes traveled across the paint-splattered marble floors and lingered with sweet melancholia on Alex's easel, which supported an untouched canvas set up in preparation for his friend's next burst of creativity.

"You will *never* be as rich as I am, dear boy." Charles put one companionable arm across his shoulder and kissed him on the ear. "It takes generations to become that wealthy and you, my love, are entirely too young—as the twinges in my lower back remind me every morning that you wake up all bright-eyed and bushy-tailed and, as we used to say back in the old days, hot to trot."

"But it's a start, right?" Corey kept looking around the room. There was still an airy boyishness about him but a new quality, something more mature and purposeful, was beginning to emerge.

Charles released him and went to perch on the foot of the bed. "Why this sudden obsession with wealth? You never cared about money before. At least, not so long as you had enough to get by."

"I still don't," Corey replied offhandedly as his gaze drifted upwards. "This whole thing with Alex and Tony, I dunno. Life is kind of short, isn't it?"

"A clichéd platitude but truer words were never spoken."

"I do have a business degree from college, you know. That's where I met Alex."

"As you've told me many times."

"I'm just thinking, maybe I should put it to use. You know, do something with my life?"

"Do something?" Charles feigned shocked surprise. "Dear, sweet child. I have more money than Midas. You needn't *do* anything other than sit around and look pretty if that's what you want."

"That's just it," Corey fretted. "I don't think that's what I want anymore. The clubs, the parties, the drinking, even the hot guys. They all seem so, I dunno, meaningless now."

"What old movie did you clip that speech from?"

Corey grinned and launched himself at the older man, bearing him backward onto the bed until he was trapped beneath his weight. He kissed him deeply and when he was done, licked the end of his nose mischievously. "I've had some great sex in my time, Charles."

"I don't doubt it."

"And you are not the best, old man. I want you to know that. *Alex* was the best."

Charles couldn't help breaking into a grin of his own and said, with mock gravity, "Far be it from me to disparage the departed. Competition is impossible, so I will gallantly cede the title of Best to our dear friend."

"But you… You, Charles…" Corey playfully loosened the banker's tie and undid the first few buttons of his starched shirt so he could plant a few light kisses on his throat. "You are pretty fucking amazing for an old goat."

"*Baaaaa,*" was Charles's only reply.

Corey moved off of him and lay at his side, head propped up on one arm. "I still can't believe Alex left everything to me."

"Except the paintings."

Corey dismissed the artwork. "They would have ended up with Nadine anyway. I wouldn't have known what to do with them." His free hand casually played with the gray hair of Charles's chest, exposed by the open collar. "She's welcome to them, for all I care. Everything Tony had went to Alex and everything Alex had, he gave me. Hey!" A thought seemed to strike him. "I can even afford to take *you* on vacation now, can't I?"

"Around the world, my precious. Around the world."

Corey frowned. "Around the world? You know what that means, don't you?"

Charles looked at him blankly.

"It's an old hooker's term. It means, well, why don't I just show you?"

He grabbed both sides of the front of Charles's shirt and yanked it open, ripping a couple of buttons off in the process. Looking down at his lover's exposed torso, he marveled again how much different it was than the tightly muscled, gym-toned bodies he'd shared beds, floors and hotel rooms with for so long. Charles was by no means decrepit, or even out of shape, but he was practically Social Security age and in spots, it showed. His stomach was still flat, but his waist had pleasing handles— Corey loved grabbing onto them when they were having sex. True, his skin was not supple, his face was lined, his balls were even a little bit saggy—but his cock! If he'd known how large an older man's cock could be, how comfortably it could fit into all those special places, and how many interesting techniques a lover could learn with age, he'd have long ago sworn off taking anyone under the age of sixty into his bed.

For years, Charles had been there for him, patiently waiting in the wings for Corey to get himself into some awful mess and need his help. No matter how screwed up Corey had gotten, no matter how many evictions, how many repossessed cars, empty bank accounts or, a couple of times, no matter how many tequila shots he'd had before pounding on the multi-millionaire's door in the middle of the night looking for someplace to sleep, Charles had always taken care of him. Nor did Corey ever feel like he was being "kept." Charles's bounty did not come without a price. Sometimes, it was a lecture on responsibility. More often, it was only through Charles's insistence that Corey was forced to own up to whatever mistakes he'd made and, with his older lover's guidance, he would try his best to make amends.

In the beginning, and probably for quite a few years afterwards, Corey would have had to honestly admit to himself, he'd looked upon Charles as a mere convenience, as a familiar port in which to take shelter from whatever storm was brewing around him. But Charles was ever kind and always supportive without ever being indulgent. Though he spoiled him utterly with clothes and jewelry and fancy dinners, Corey didn't have an entitled bone in his body, and he never became uppity or demanding and he never even came close to becoming a spoiled brat.

It was one of the many reasons Charles loved him.

And to Corey's surprise, during the past few weeks, he'd realized how much he loved Charles in return—how much he'd *always* loved him without knowing it or truly understanding what the emotion was.

It took inheriting Alex's fortune to bring him to that conclusion. With so much money of his own, he had no monetary reason to stick around in Charles's house. He could easily afford one of his own—perhaps with a swimming pool so he could have round-the-clock parties with gorgeous young studs in swimsuits which barely covered their dicks lying out around it or lined up at the twenty-four-hour open bar he'd always imagined would be part of the scenario. But he'd delayed moving out; even after he'd gotten the keys to both the old townhouse and the new condo, he'd stayed with Charles.

He enjoyed the older man's company, and he *adored* the sex. The thought of coming home at night without Charles there, the idea of sharing those expensive meals in restaurants with anyone else, the prospect of not having Charles tucked into his favorite armchair reading his boring financial papers when Corey was stricken with the impulse to share some incredibly profound thought—well, profound to Corey—filled him with a sense of deep sadness and loss. Irrespective of the financial security he represented, Charles was good company. He was comfortable to be with. He was safe. He adored Corey and, above all, Corey finally accepted, he was loved.

He rested his head against Charles's bare chest and sighed with contentment. His fingers explored lower until they reached his lover's belt. Impatiently, he began tugging at it to remove it.

"We have company, you know. Won't we feel like exhibitionists?"

Corey stopped, puzzled. Realization dawned when he saw Charles was looking at the statues, all of them gazing fondly down at them.

"They are beautiful, aren't they?" Corey commented.

Charles's only response was a grunt of agreement.

"I don't think, no matter how much Nadine would have wanted them, I could have given them up. I don't know why, or what it was, but they *meant* something to Alex. The minute he saw them, I could tell he thought they were special."

"Which is your favorite?" Charles wanted to know. "I'm partial to the Capricorn, of course, but perhaps that's just because I own the painting."

"Dunno. The guy with the ring in his nose and the one with the horns have the biggest dicks, don't they?"

"You're obsessed, child. Do you know that? But yes, I agree that Taurus and Aries are particularly well endowed."

"I think the slender guy with the long hair—that would be Leo, right? I think him and Scorpio are probably the winners for plain old raw sexiness. But the young boy in the corner?"

"Virgo, I think."

"Yeah. He's supposed to be a virgin, isn't he? There's something about him that just sort of makes you wanna lick him all over and make his eyes go all bulgy when he gets turned on for the first time. I guess..." He paused, considering. "I don't have a favorite. I like 'em all."

He snuggled in closer to Charles and the two lay in silence for a few moments, each lost in their own thoughts. They were sad for their loss, but the wounds had grown less ragged during the past weeks. Their pain wasn't quite as acute and they could look back on the two men they had known and loved with fond remembrance and not a little melancholia.

"Alex had a favorite, though." Corey's voice, low and almost sleepy, broke the quiet.

"Did he?" Charles was intrigued. "Which?"

"There." Corey pointed and Charles followed his finger. "The Twins."

"Gemini? That's not what I would have thought. They're stunning, of course, but...Gemini wasn't Alex's birth sign, was it?"

"Dunno. All I know is that he was always kind of taken with them. He told me the day I helped him move in. He said that even though they were twins, he didn't think of them as brothers. Well, not birth brothers anyway. He thought they were more like lovers who were a single soul split up into two bodies."

"Perhaps a little overly romantic for my taste," Charles said without criticism. "But I understand what he meant. Go on."

"'Romantic' was the word he used. The two of them, always together. See how their hands are on each other's dicks and somehow, the fingers sort of sink in? When Alex got up on a ladder to fix the skylight, he took a closer look. You can't see it from this angle, but each one's arm goes into the other one's shoulder where they're sort of holding on to each other. And their hips and thighs are joined, too."

"Always together. Captured in marble forever."

"That's exactly how Alex put it!"

"Like you and me, eh, youngster?"

"I dunno," Corey teased. "What happens if some even older man comes along and I fall madly in love and he steals me away from you?"

"We will cross that bridge, my love," Charles kissed Corey deeply before continuing, their tongues playing tag with each other, "when we come to it. And, if such a thing *ever* happens…"

"Yeah?"

"I will use every last penny I have to hunt down this stealer of lovers and haul you back to me, making sure in the process that his body is never found."

Corey giggled for a moment and then grew somber. "Speaking of never being found, do you ever wonder…"

"All the time, my dear. All the time."

Corey looked back up at the Gemini. "I never really noticed it before, but don't you think it's strange?"

"What?"

"The Twins. One of them seems lighter than the other. I'll betcha if they were real, he'd be a blond. And d'you wanna know the oddest thing? For some weird reason, they remind me of Alex and Tony. It's not that they look anything like them. There's just something about them that seems, I dunno, familiar. Don't you think?"

"I think," Charles said, "since my shirt is already open and my pants half undone, that it's terribly unfair that *you* are still fully clothed."

In scant moments, the two men lay naked in each other's arms.

Above them, each melded to the other, the shadows across the faces of the Gemini gave them the flickering appearance of life. Their handsome faces seemed to smile down upon the lovers with approval. Unnoticed by the two on the bed, the marble statues moved, almost imperceptibly, closer together and the air surrounding them shimmered. Their heads turned slightly so it seemed as if they were gazing deeply into each other's eyes.

Neither Corey nor Charles looked up, so absorbed were they in their explorations of each other's bodies. Even if they had, they would have been likely to have missed it. There, on the chest of the young man Corey had thought would be blond, a small splotch of blue paint appeared momentarily and then faded. A similar speck of red graced one thigh and a tiny speckle of yellow marred one marble arm. For several moments, colors appeared on the statue's skin, glistening as if they were still-wet oils from a painter's palette, absently wiped from a hand too busily absorbed in creation to bother using a rag.

By the time Corey and Charles were finished, lying in drowsy surfeited repose, and thought to cast their eyes up once again, all traces of paint were gone. The marble was as smooth and white and unblemished as they had thought it had been.

Alex and Tony stood, looking down on them fondly. Though they shared in the joy of their friends' newfound romance, they could not spend much time on it.

They were too absorbed in other things.

In loving each other.

About the Author

Hal Bodner is the author of the best-selling gay vampire novel, *Bite Club* and the lupine sequel, *The Trouble With Hairy*. He tells people that he was born in East Philadelphia because no one knows where Cherry Hill, New Jersey is. The obstetrician who delivered him was C. Everett Coop, the future U.S. Surgeon General who put warnings on cigarette packs. Thus, from birth, Hal was destined to become a heavy smoker.

He moved to West Hollywood in the 1980s and has rarely left the city limits since. He cannot even find his way around Beverly Hills—which is the next town over.

Hal has been an entertainment lawyer, a scheduler for a 976 sex telephone line, a theater reviewer and the personal assistant to a television star. For a while, he owned Heavy Petting, a pet boutique where all the movie stars shopped for their Pomeranians. Until recently, he owned an exotic bird shop.

He has never been a waiter.

He lives with assorted dogs, and birds, the most notable of which is an eighty year old irritable, flesh-eating military macaw named after his icon—Tallulah. He often quips he is a slave to fur and feathers and regrets only that he isn't referring to mink and marabou. He does not have cats because he tends to sneeze on them.

Having reached middle-age, he remembers Nixon.

He was widowed in his early forties and can sometimes be found sunbathing at his late partner's grave while trying to avoid cemetery caretakers screaming at him to put his shirt back on.

Hal has also written a few erotic paranormal romances,

which he refers to as "supernatural smut"—most notably In *Flesh and Stone* and *For Love of the Dead*. While his salacious imagination is unbounded, he much prefers his comedic roots and he is currently pecking away at a series of bitterly humorous gay super hero novels.

He married again—this time legally—to a wonderful man who is young enough not to know that Liza Minnelli is Judy Garland's daughter. As a result, Hal has recently discovered that the use of hair dye is rarely an adequate substitute for Viagra.

Hal's website is www.wehovampire.com and he encourages fans to send him email at Hal@wehovampire.com. It may take him a month or so, but he generally responds to almost everyone who writes to him with the sole exception of prisoners who request free copies of his books accompanied by naked pictures.

Watch for Hal's newest titles coming soon:

FABULOUS IN TIGHTS

The adventures of the Whirlwind, a reluctant superhero...

and the sequel:

A STUDY IN SPANDEX.

Curious about other Crossroad Press books?
Stop by our site:
http://store.crossroadpress.com
We offer quality writing
in digital, audio, and print formats.

9 781952 979897